SPECIAL MESSAGE TO READERS

THE ULVERSCROFT FOUNDATION

(registered UK charity number 264873)

was established in 1972 to provide funds for research, diagnosis and treatment of eye diseases. Examples of major projects funded by the Ulverscroft Foundation are:

- The Children's Eye Unit at Moorfields Eye Hospital, London
- The Ulverscroft Children's Eye Unit at Great Ormond Street Hospital for Sick Children
- Funding research into eye diseases and treatment at the Department of Ophthalmology, University of Leicester
- The Ulverscroft Vision Research Group, Institute of Child Health
- Twin operating theatres at the Western Ophthalmic Hospital, London
- The Chair of Ophthalmology at the Royal Australian College of Ophthalmologists

You can help further the work of the Foundation by making a donation or leaving a legacy. Every contribution is gratefully received. If you would like to help support the Foundation or require further information, please contact:

THE ULVERSCROFT FOUNDATION
The Green, Bradgate Road, Anstey
Leicester LE7 7FU, England
Tel: (0116) 236 4325
website: www.ulverscroft-foundation.org.uk

RISKY BUSINESS

It seems odd that Letty's boss is so keen for her to learn the outmoded skill of shorthand. But when her teacher Miss Kemp suffers a serious fall, Letty's skill and eye for detail lead her — along with Miss Kemp's gorgeous nephew Adam — into finding clues to a decades-old crime. And that could put them both, and their friends, in grave danger . . .

GAIL RICHARDS

RISKY BUSINESS

Complete and Unabridged

LINFORD ROMANCE

LINFORD
Leicester

First published in Great Britain in 2020

First Linford Edition
published 2023

A catalogue record for this book is available from the British Library.

ISBN 978–1–4448–5004–8

Published by
Ulverscroft Limited
Anstey, Leicestershire

Printed and bound in Great Britain by
TJ Books Ltd., Padstow, Cornwall

This book is printed on acid-free paper

1

Letty stood in the lobby tugging at the gate. It wouldn't budge.

She'd never quite trusted this lift, always sighing with relief when she reached her destination, the top floor. But her apprehension at getting in was always mixed with anticipation as she clanked her way up to Miss Kemp's flat, and her shorthand lesson.

Now she glanced at her phone. Still a couple of minutes till her lesson time. She could walk up.

Brisk footsteps on the stairs made her step back, and a young man strode into the lobby.

'Are you trying to call the lift?' he asked, seeing her standing there. 'Have another go. Someone had left the gate open on the first floor — I've closed it now.'

Letty pulled again at the gate and it slid open in the way it usually did.

'Thanks. You've saved me a long walk up.'

He was very attractive, with light brown hair swept back from a smooth brow and warm, brown eyes. Letty felt a disconcerting flutter.

He seemed to hesitate and for a moment she thought he was going to say something else — ask for her phone number maybe.

No. He was waiting for her to get into the lift so he could close the gates for her.

She wouldn't have given her number, of course. Would she? On the basis of thirty seconds' contact and a feeling when he smiled at her?

'I'll report the fault,' he said as she stepped in. 'Alarms should have gone off.'

Letty nodded encouragingly. 'Yes — good idea.'

Miss Kemp was slim and lively, but Letty wondered how she'd manage the stairs as she got older if this sort of thing happened again.

The young man started to close the gate behind Letty.

'Do you live here?'

'No. Do you?'

He was smiling. 'No. But I visit often.' He seemed reluctant to allow the lift to go. 'Do you?'

'I'm here at this time every week.'

He nodded and closed the gate. Her last sight was of a pair of brown eyes twinkling.

That would have to do. Today's lesson hadn't even started, and Letty was already looking forward to next Thursday.

* * *

Miss Kemp looked cheerful when she opened the door, with her neat Judi Dench haircut and a small bead necklace around the collar of her crisp white blouse.

Letty sat where she always sat, on one side of the big desk, notebook in front of her. On Miss Kemp's side were books and dictionaries. In the middle was a pot of pencils and a sharpener.

Miss Kemp smiled as usual.

'Evening, Letty. How has your week been?'

Letty pulled a rueful face. Her boss had asked her to learn shorthand and she wanted to do well, despite practically no one else learning this old-fashioned note-taking method.

'My boss's PA made me sit in a meeting with her and take notes. It was only one speaker she wanted me to focus on but I didn't feel ready.'

'Did you cope?'

'Not really. While I was going back over some of the shorthand notes I'd made and filling in gaps in longhand, the rest were still talking so when my guy piped up again, I had no idea what he was saying.'

Miss Kemp smiled. 'It does help if you can keep track of what's going on. How much did you manage to type out afterwards?'

'That was hard as well. I didn't know

whether to go with what the outline looked like regardless of whether the sentence made sense or not, or make something up even if my outline was nothing like it.' Letty shrugged, remembering her doubts.

'Your outlines are quite precise, Letty. You should usually be able to trust yourself, but throwing you in before you're ready wasn't kind.'

'Maria isn't kind.' There was no doubt there.

'Oh, that was said with feeling,' Miss Kemp remarked.

'She's been in that office for way longer than me and as far as I know, has always been the only one who's known shorthand. She's asked to do a lot of ultra-confidential stuff where she shreds her pages afterwards, and triple password protected documents, and then deletes them as well. I think she's scared I'll take those jobs away from her.' Letty sighed. 'I feel like telling her she's welcome to all that. I'd hate to be involved in undercover stuff. Anyway,' she added, 'after this week's attempt she'll realise I'm not a threat.'

'It didn't turn out well?'

'There were a lot of gaps. Is that right about my outlines being precise?'

Miss Kemp smiled. 'Except for the little trademark flourish you do on your -s plurals that anyone else may mistake for something else — but you know that's how you do it.'

'A flourish? Do I? What's your trademark?'

That made the teacher laugh.

'People have complained my mark for capital letters is unclear. They mistake it for something else, or nothing — but I know.'

She got up to turn lamps on and the one over a shelf on one of the walls flashed on, then with a ping went out. She went over to the drawer and took out a light bulb.

'I think it's one of these,' she said. 'They're all different now, aren't they?'

'I'll do it,' Letty offered. She slipped her shoes off and began pulling a chair over to the wall.

'Not like that, Letty. It's too easy to wobble and fall from a chair. I've got a little step ladder.'

She pointed to a cupboard in the hallway. Soon Letty had the old bulb out and was trying to put the new one in.

'There's something wrong with the fitting. It's not going in.'

'Let's leave it for now. There's enough light.' Miss Kemp put the old bulb on the shelf and went back to her desk. 'The same thing happened to the other one not long ago. I think they must both be very old. I'll get them both sorted out eventually, but there's no hurry.'

'How long have you lived here, Miss Kemp?' Letty asked as she folded up the ladder and returned it to its cupboard.

'Six, seven months,' Miss Kemp said vaguely.

That was a surprise. Letty had imagined Miss Kemp living here for decades. She went back to her own place at the desk.

'Now, show me your homework.' Miss

Kemp reached out for Letty's notebook. 'And have you been doing any reading?'

'It's slow going,' Letty confessed.

'Yes.' Miss Kemp's eyes twinkled, as they often did, and today it made Letty think with a lurch of her insides about the man she'd met on the way up. 'But is it slow going because it's in shorthand or because it's Conan Doyle?'

'I know what you mean. He's not going to be one of my favourites.'

'I sometimes think perhaps I should translate a more modern book. Would someone like Stephen King be an easier read?'

'Marian Keyes,' Letty said and Miss Kemp nodded thoughtfully while Letty continued. 'I was sitting on the train trying to read some of the Sherlock Holmes and the man next to me was peering over. As he got off, he couldn't help himself — he asked if it was Arabic.'

'I expect he was pleased he was getting off when you told him. He would be embarrassed.'

Letty laughed with Miss Kemp and as

her teacher looked over her homework, glanced along the shelves behind her, and then around the room. It was comforting, the way everything was always the same here.

It wasn't only the old-fashioned lift, it was sitting here learning something no one learned any more as if it was the 1970s, taught by someone who could have been Letty's own age in the 1970s.

Even her mum had laughed.

'It's the twenty-first century,' she'd said. 'Nobody does shorthand any more. Aren't there more useful skills they could teach you?'

'What can I say? I've got an eccentric boss,' Letty said. 'Anyway, it's interesting. And it's useful when someone's speaking too fast on the phone and you need to take a message.'

In addition, Miss Kemp's flat was like a quiet and cheerful haven and the teacher herself made her feel secure. You could block out any tension from the real world.

Letty was making the best of her

employment situation but sometimes wished she was back at the charity she'd worked for that had been so madly busy, no one noticed the finances weren't stacking up until it was too late.

After the announcement that they couldn't continue, Letty took the first job that came her way — Nate Wickham Accountancy Services. She thought it was supplying a service and giving advice. Now she was beginning to think it mainly involved making money and keeping secrets.

To start with she was sorry she hadn't waited for something better, but now she was getting used to it. There was an element of risk either way — taking a job you might not like, or ending up without a job.

Would shorthand be a good skill to have on her CV when she updated it? Letty doubted it. But she had Miss Kemp's flat to go to on Thursdays . . . and now she had the excitement of looking forward to seeing that man again next week.

* * *

Letty was still surprised every time she walked into her new workplace. It was all plush carpet and immaculate fittings — nothing like the little charity she'd worked for before, where nothing matched and the paintwork had seen better days. That office had been housed in a warren of a building and the only way up was via a bare wooden staircase. In this modern building, a silent lift whizzed you up in seconds and the doors purred as they opened to let you out.

Nate Wickham's company was a small concern, which had been one of the things that attracted her after she'd been happy in the cosy atmosphere of the charity. There, people had helped one another out when needed. But she barely understood what any of the others did in the new place, let alone felt able to offer them any assistance.

Her boss, Nate himself, had a room at the end of an open-plan office. You never knew whether he was there or not, and had to knock at the door and wait till he said 'Come in'. She and his PA, Maria Palmer, sat outside, shielded by a shoulder-high screen from the dozen or so other workers.

When Letty had started they gave her a desk facing Maria, adjoining Maria's desk in the middle. Although Letty's was smaller, Maria would irritably push away anything of Letty's that strayed on to her compulsively tidy workspace.

'Would it be all right if I turned my desk to face the window?' Letty asked after a week or so. 'The light's making it difficult to see my screen.'

That wasn't the only reason. Letty was aware Maria was surreptitiously watching everything Letty did. She wasn't doing anything wrong — indeed, was doing everything Nate asked and more — but being watched made her uncomfortable. Besides, it made her cringe to see Maria leap up to pander to the boss's every wish. It was so undignified.

Maria clearly didn't like Letty much

either, and probably didn't want to sit looking at her. The new arrangement wouldn't stop Maria checking up on her — but so long as Letty wasn't aware of it every minute, she didn't mind so much.

Better still, now Letty had a view of the sky and was becoming fascinated by the way it changed. She loved watching how fast the clouds moved some days. It made her feel excited, as though outside there was a fast-moving world where anything would be possible.

The fatal flaw in her plan, which she didn't think of until she'd heaved the desk round and struggled with the cables, was that anyone could creep up behind her. And they often waited until she had a cup of coffee in her hand.

'Letty?' This time it was Claire from the open-plan office. 'Oh, sorry. I didn't mean to make you jump. You need a rear view mirror.'

Letty swivelled in her chair, smiling. Claire, the office manager, was the person she got on with best in the workplace.

'I'm thinking of hanging a row of windchimes people will have to walk through that would warn me someone's coming.' Letty glanced up at the high ceiling. 'That would work, wouldn't it?'

'It would make you very popular, I'm sure.' Claire nodded towards the boss's office. 'Where are they?'

'They?'

'The chiefs.'

There was a definite pecking order in this company. Claire worked closely with the deputy, Terry, but according to Claire he was not in Nate Wickham's confidence. Terry had to balance the books often without knowing what was planned, or by collating information from as many of the consultants as he could. It all seemed rather vague to Letty, and not particularly businesslike. Maria was in the know, and Letty had the impression that Claire and Terry both wanted information about what went on in the secret meetings where Maria took shorthand notes. Letty liked Claire, but didn't have any details to share even if she'd wanted to.

'Nate's seeing some clients — and didn't I see Terry earlier?' she said.

'I meant Nate and Maria.' Claire laughed. 'I don't really count Terry as one of the bosses.'

So Maria was considered to be one of the bosses? That was weird. Letty would never have thought of her that way.

'I don't think they're necessarily together,' Letty said. 'When Nate's out seeing what he calls his high net worth clients, if Maria's out at the same time they don't usually come back together. I always think she must be somewhere else because no one is allowed to get near that group of clients.' Letty thought about it. 'Maybe she's making the most of him not being around?'

'No. I'd be very surprised if Maria had anything in her life apart from this company.'

'Mmm, as soon as I said it I realised it wasn't likely. I wouldn't consider her one of the bosses, though. Even if Terry does seem to be sidelined a lot of the time.'

'He actually sent me to try to find out what he's being excluded from this time.'

'I wish I could help. I'm excluded myself.'

'Yes, he knows that but he wondered if Nate might have mentioned who he was seeing today.'

'No — sorry.'

Wait. Terry knew she was excluded from some of the things that went on at this end of the office?

'Terry talks about me?'

Letty was fond of portly, middle-aged Terry, who had adopted six children and appeared to be a very caring father despite the different troubles each of the six seemed to have brought with them. That was probably why he hadn't done better in this company — you had to be more single-minded.

'He let slip that he hoped you don't get *sucked in*,' Claire said. 'He thinks you're too decent to get mixed up in some of what Nate does.'

'Really? What does Nate do that's so bad?'

'He clammed up after that. I think it's to do with the way he gets clients sometimes, elbowing other companies out of the way.'

'Doesn't everyone do that?' Letty said. 'The whole world's become pretty cut-throat.'

'Terry thinks there are degrees of being competitive, and Nate . . .'

'Goes a bit far?' Letty had wondered that herself. 'I wonder if he's successful because he's friendly and sociable. People like him.'

'I really like having you here — but maybe you should leave while you're still innocent and clean.'

'What — he's not just charismatic and a good salesman?'

Claire frowned. Letty continued.

'This is serious talk, Claire. Has Terry convinced you I'm in danger of being contaminated? Is that what happened to Maria?'

Her colleague shook her head. 'No — Maria has been here right from when the company was first set up.'

'How long ago was that?'

'Nineteen, twenty years? Terry was one of the first to join, and he was single then.'

'Nate must have been quite young then,' Letty said. 'And Maria too.'

'Yes, Terry was older. He still is.' Claire giggled. 'His problem is, he hasn't kept his accounting skills up to date, and methods and regulations are all changing so quickly. Plus now everything's digitised and he got pushed aside in favour of kids who grew up doing everything online.'

'Nate's done well to keep up, then — and to run the IT side.'

'You admire him, don't you?'

Letty hesitated.

'I can see why you would.'

'He is . . . *attractive*, isn't he?'

'Be careful, Letty.'

'No, no — not like that.' Letty remembered the man by the lift at Miss Kemp's and knew she would never in a million years see Nate as a romantic interest. He was middle-aged!

It was too soon to tell Claire that there

might be a new man in her life. Nothing may come of it. She had to be very sure this time.

She'd had a boyfriend when she worked at the charity, but when all the staff went their separate ways he left town without a backward glance. She supposed it had been convenient to have a girlfriend at work, when much of your socialising was with work colleagues. Letty had lost her job, her social life and her boyfriend in one go.

'I'm going to stick around for a full year so it doesn't look too bad on my CV and then find something better,' she confided. 'Are you OK working here, though?'

Claire was probably ten years older than Letty. She must be in her mid-thirties and had been with the company since she was around Letty's current age — always in the same position.

Letty wondered if she just wasn't ambitious. It didn't seem likely she was in love with Terry — anyone less like a romantic hero was difficult to imagine — but of course you could never know the ways of the human heart.

'I'm sort of allowed to do what I like, so long as I don't spend too much money, so it's good experience.' Claire hesitated. 'Plus Terry's kind of painted himself into a corner and needs this job. I really like his wife as well. The whole family. I get a lot of satisfaction working with him.'

'You're shielding him from the worst excesses of the bosses?' 'Not sure I'm that powerful — but, yeah, something like that.'

As she watched Claire walk away Letty reflected that it could simply be that Claire had chosen a safe life. For herself, there was something exciting about working at this end of the office. Exciting and dangerous — and, despite herself, that appealed to her.

2

Letty took the stairs the next Thursday evening. It was a risk either way. The man she hoped to see might take the lift this week, and they would miss one another.

Or he may walk down from a lower floor, and she could pass it before he started down.

Or she could have mistimed it altogether . . .

As she embarked on the last flight of stairs, she could hear voices on the sixth floor. Two male voices. Her spirits rose. She slowed down, so as not to be out of breath when she saw him.

Even with easing her pace, Letty felt breathless at the sight of the man from the week before when she reached the top of the staircase.

He was even more handsome than she'd remembered. How was that possible? But not quite as tall — which was good, because Letty wasn't tall herself.

Or it could be that the other man was taller. The policeman . . .

Letty's cheerful greeting died in her throat when she saw how serious the two of them looked.

The lift announced itself with a ping and the men nodded at one another as the police officer stepped in.

The young man turned to Letty as the policeman began to clank his way down.

'You're not my Aunt Rowena's student, are you?'

'Miss Kemp?'

He nodded. 'There's been an accident. She's in hospital.'

'Oh! That's a shock. What happened?'

'We don't know.'

There was an awkward silence and Letty wondered whether she should call for the lift.

He nodded towards the door to Miss Kemp's flat. 'Do you want to come in for a minute? I'm Adam Taylor,' he said as they made their way in.

She nodded. 'Letty Wood. What's wrong with Miss Kemp?'

'She fell,' Adam said.

Letty sat at her usual side of the table. It was now empty, except for the pot of pencils and the sharpener that were always there.

'What — here in the flat?' Letty asked.

He nodded.

'The neighbour opposite took a parcel in for her yesterday and kept knocking to hand it over but there was no answer. This morning she called the police.'

'And did the police come round? I'm surprised they'd get involved.'

'The poor neighbour was beside herself. She kept saying, 'Rowena wouldn't have ordered books and then gone off without telling me'.'

Letty nodded. 'I bet that's true. She's very — proper, your aunt.'

Adam smiled. 'She is. Anyway, they got hold of the property management company and someone came round with a key and there she was, lying on the floor.'

'Oh, no. Had she been there for twenty-four hours?' That was shocking.

'We think so. She had a real bump on her head and was dehydrated. She's in intensive care.'

'Has she been able to explain what happened?'

'She hasn't come round yet.'

'Poor Miss Kemp . . .'

Adam looked at her as if seeing her properly for the first time. 'You're fond of her, aren't you?'

Letty looked over his head to avoid staring into his eyes. She did want to, but they would distract her, and this was serious.

'She's gentle and kind,' she said. 'She doesn't deserve to suffer like this.'

Adam gave a sad smile and despite her determination it wouldn't happen, held her gaze.

Confused, she looked away. That was odd — Miss Kemp's shelves didn't look as neat as usual. She wondered if her tutor tidied up before her pupils arrived. She'd always imagined her to be naturally well ordered.

She pushed down the niggle in her

head and glanced back at Adam, then around the rest of the room. 'I wonder how she hit her head so badly just by falling,' she said.

He nodded towards the light fittings on the wall by the shelves. 'The police think she was standing on a chair to change a light bulb. They found the bulb that had gone.'

'Those lights don't work,' Letty said, and Adam looked surprised. 'Anyway, Miss Kemp doesn't stand on chairs to do anything like that. She's got a step ladder.'

Adam laughed and despite his obvious worry, it lit up his face. He put a hand up to run through his hair. She let her glance stray to his bare ring finger.

'And you know all this how?' he asked.

'When I was here last week, the bulb went on one of them — the other one hadn't worked for ages, she told me. So I said I'd change it. I started to get up on a chair and she lectured me about health and safety so I got her steps out.'

'You're right. There's no way she'd

climb on a chair.'

'Anyway the light fitting is totally broken — it wasn't the bulb. Or it might have been, but I couldn't get a new one in. And the other lamp's the same. She said she'd get someone in to look at them but it wasn't a priority.'

'What did she do with the old light bulb last week?'

'She left it there.' Letty pointed to the shelf under the two lamps. 'If the police think that's what happened, they're wrong.'

'Yes!' Adam looked happier. 'I knew that was a strange story.'

They sat looking at one another for a moment.

'So what did happen?' Letty said.

After a moment's thought Adam looked at his watch and Letty's heart sank. It was terrible that Miss Kemp had had an accident but Adam was so pleasant to be with, despite the flutter she sometimes felt when she looked at him — or because of it — and they seemed to be getting on.

Besides, she really wanted to get to the bottom of what had happened to her nice teacher.

'I promised the woman across the hall I'd knock for a chat,' Adam said. 'I don't want to leave it too late.'

Letty stood up. 'Sure. She seems like a good neighbour to your aunt.'

Adam remained seated for a moment longer, looking up at Letty.

'I would like . . . I don't want . . .' He couldn't seem to finish the thought.

'Shall we exchange phone numbers and email addresses?' Even if that wasn't what he was trying to say, he could message her and that might be easier. 'I'd really like to know how your aunt's doing.'

Adam got his phone out. 'Yes, let's do that. Um,' he added, looking at it. Letty wasn't sure whether he was flushing or not. 'Maybe we could go out for a drink,' he added. 'Saturday perhaps.'

'That would be lovely.'

Adam carried on smiling while he gave her his number and email address and took Letty's. Then he stood up, seeming reluctant.

'I don't know what I'm going to say to the neighbour,' he said. 'There's nothing to tell.'

'Would you like me to go in with you?'

Adam hesitated and Letty immediately regretted offering.

'All right,' he said.

* * *

The kindly woman in the other flat introduced herself as Eva when Letty explained who she was. Eva led them into a cosy lounge crowded with furniture and Letty found herself sitting side by side with Adam on a two-seater sofa. He sat on the edge of his seat so Letty leaned forward.

'How is Rowena?' The woman plumped herself down opposite them.

'She's still in intensive care.'

'Have you found out what happened?'

'No, she hasn't been able to speak yet. Do you have any idea? She didn't talk about — I don't know, dizzy spells or anything?'

'Not at all. No, I don't believe she had any health issues.'

'Do you know if she had any visitors recently? Anyone different to the usual?'

'Once we're inside we don't hear what goes on in the hallway or who visits the other flats, but . . .'

'We'd really appreciate it if you could think of anything unusual that might have happened.'

Letty saw Adam glance at her. Maybe he wanted to pursue the idea of illness or accident further but Letty wanted to rule out the possibility of an intruder — unlikely as it seemed in a block of flats like this. Anyway, the hospital would find out if there was anything physically amiss with Miss Kemp.

'Well, I sit at the window sometimes. It's quite high up so you don't see a great deal of detail but I can see who parks over the road. Not in any great detail, you understand, and I don't recognise makes of car . . .'

'What did you see?' Letty encouraged.

'There was a navy blue car parked over the road on and off for a week or two. You're not supposed to park there during the day unless you've got a resident's permit. And now there's building work going on, I'm sure you're not allowed because of site traffic needing to get in and out.' Eva gave a little laugh. 'Though to be honest I don't think there's much going on behind that fence.'

'What sort of times did you see it?'

'Various, an hour here and there.'

'Daytime?' Letty asked.

'An hour in the morning, an hour at lunchtime, that sort of thing. Then longer once the parking restrictions weren't in force.'

'Do you ever see traffic wardens here? Could it have been someone who was getting permits from someone?'

'I've never seen anyone checking. But they were sitting in the car, so would have been able to drive away if they saw a warden appear.'

'Right. Did this happen every day?'

'No, I don't think so. I don't know. But never all night, so that's why I thought they probably didn't live here.'

'What could it have been about?'

Eva laughed. 'I thought it must have been a private detective watching someone's movements. That's what it seemed like. It's just that when you asked, I thought it might be worth mentioning . . .'

'Definitely,' Letty said. 'No one got out?'

'Not that I saw. It was there once when I was on my way out, and I crossed over to try to see who was inside but the sun was shining on the windows. I didn't want to bend down to peer in.' Eva looked slightly embarrassed. 'It was probably nothing.'

Adam laughed. 'I had a friend who was buying a house and he got me to go with him a few nights to sit outside and see how noisy the street was. We must have looked well suspicious.'

Letty got up to go to the window.

'May I?' she asked. She moved the

curtain a fraction to peer out. You couldn't see much in the dark, but probably enough to recognise the same-shaped car in the same place a few times. She wondered if you'd know there was someone inside — if they moved you probably would, and when Eva crossed over the road she'd have seen. 'Have you not seen this car since?' she asked. 'You said a few weeks.'

'Well, I had plumbers in last week and it was all a bit chaotic. I wouldn't have noticed.'

'No, it's never easy having workmen in,' Letty said. 'I hope they fixed your problem.'

'I didn't know I had a problem until they knocked. They were doing something for someone downstairs and traced a fault up here. I was lucky they caught it.'

Adam caught Letty's eye with a worried glance. 'Was it just you, or did they come and knock on anyone else's door?'

'I'm not sure. I didn't speak to anyone else about it, and Rowena didn't say anything.'

'Did they charge you a lot?'

'No, it was very reasonable. And I paid through the bank account so they're paying their VAT.'

'Do you remember what they were called?' Adam still seemed worried.

'It was a two-man outfit. Frank and Cliff, their names were, so they called the company C&F Plumbers. They had cards but in the end they didn't leave me one.'

'And everything's been all right since?' Adam asked. 'You sometimes hear about unscrupulous people canvassing for work . . .'

'Yes, I've had no problems. They even tightened the loose screws in one of my door handles.'

Adam smiled. 'That's good.'

Letty really liked Adam. He had all the worry of his aunt, and yet had some concern left over for a stranger he was afraid might have been targeted by rogue traders.

'Can I just ask about this week?' Letty

asked. 'You took a parcel in for Miss Kem — for Rowena?'

'Yes. My plumbers finished on the Tuesday and this was on the Wednesday morning. The delivery people know us now, we take parcels in for one another and the other two flats on this floor. Otherwise they have to lug them back downstairs and back to their depot and they don't get much time for each drop.'

She was a nice woman. Letty hoped the plumbers hadn't taken her for a ride.

'And you kept knocking on her door to pass it on to her?'

'All the rest of yesterday, and then this morning I got worried because it's not like Rowena to go away and not let me know. She does go away occasionally, but certainly if she'd ordered something she would have told me she wouldn't be there to take it in and asked me to hold on to it for her. She knows I fret about having other people's parcels for too long.'

'You know one another well,' Letty said.

'Well, no, I wouldn't say so, but we're good neighbours.'

'Didn't Rowena tell me once you had one another's keys for emergencies?' Adam said.

'We did. At least, she's still got mine, but hers isn't where it always was. I've been racking my brain to try to remember when I gave it back — sometimes if she has someone to stay, she asks for it. She must have kept it from the last time that happened but I can't remember when it would have been.' Eva looked distressed. 'So annoying, because I could have gone in earlier and got help for her.'

'Does anyone else know you keep one another's keys?' Letty asked.

Eva gave a little shrug and made a face to say she had no idea. 'The meter reader, I suppose. And the building management people.'

Letty nodded. Potentially everyone in the block, then. She didn't even know what she was trying to prove. She sat back for a moment while Adam wound up the visit, then got up with him and said her own thanks and goodbyes to Eva.

Adam was thoughtful too as they left, and he walked ahead of her slowly towards the lift. Of course, it would be awkward if she went back into Miss Kemp's flat, and she'd have the problem of gauging the time she would have to leave. Far better to go now. They had one another's numbers. They'd confirm their date for Saturday and fix the details later.

Please let the lift be busy going down, she thought.

Adam turned to her. 'Well, I don't know what we found out in there.' He looked very tired as he reached up to press the button to call the lift.

'I wanted poor Eva to have the solution.' She laughed. 'I expect Miss Kemp will wake up tomorrow and tell us everything.' She paused. 'Tell *you* everything.' She was making assumptions when she'd told herself she wouldn't. Anyway, he seemed anxious to see her on her way.

'I do hope you're right.'

Letty watched for Adam to give her a smile as the gates closed but he nodded to her and turned immediately to go back into his aunt's flat. This was very different to last week when she'd seen his twinkling eyes as she got into the lift, something she'd cherished all week.

She wished with all her heart she hadn't gone into the neighbour's flat with him. Before that he was keen on seeing her on Saturday. What had happened to make him dismiss her like that, without even a smile?

3

'Coming up behind you, Letty.' How thoughtful. She wouldn't need wind-chimes if everyone was as considerate as her boss this Monday morning.

If only Adam had been thoughtful enough to at least answer her friendly text reminding him they'd agreed to meet at the weekend.

They had, hadn't they? But even if she'd got that wrong, he could have updated her on Miss Kemp's condition.

'Morning, Nate,' she said, swivelling round.

'Maria's not coming in this morning,' Nate said. 'And I have an important meeting.'

Letty's heart sank. Even if she'd slept well the night before, which she hadn't, she was reluctant to take notes at an important meeting.

'Don't panic, Letty. I just need you to write down the main points of agreement.

My memory's not bad but my scrawl is hard to read at the best of times.'

Letty smiled. 'I know.'

Nate gave her a smile too. He really was a good boss, self-deprecating and supportive. 'Yes, you do know that. And it's hard to get everything down and think of the next thing you need to say.'

'Sure. But how do I know what the main points are? Wouldn't one of the other consultants be better?'

Nate's smile disappeared and Letty was afraid she'd gone too far.

Plus, she wasn't entirely useless. She'd be able to work out what the main points were even if it wasn't clear what they meant.

'Sorry,' she said hastily. 'Of course I'll do it.'

'You'll know the main points when you hear them,' Nate said. 'And I trust you more than the others not to gossip about what you hear.'

Nate was keeping secrets from the other staff?

He showed her where to sit at the big,

round table and left to go down and fetch the clients.

A round table was interesting — no one more important than anyone else, no one in an out-of-the-way position. Surely this showed her boss was inclusive and didn't want to put himself above anyone else?

When the visitors arrived there were only four of them, all men in their thirties and forties in suits. They introduced themselves and Letty scribbled down names and job titles.

While they outlined what they wanted from Nate and he told them what was wrong with what they were asking for, Letty had a chance to sort out who was most important, so that if he or Nate said something definitive she knew this was more likely to need to be noted.

She didn't think this company could be one of Nate's high net worth clients — as if anyone was better than someone else because they had more money! Nate always saw them out of the office, so she wouldn't have a chance to find out what it was about them that made them special.

Every now and then she wrote something in her mix of long and shorthand and felt Nate alongside her give a little nod. Other times he would glance at her and she'd write what he repeated.

None of it seemed at all controversial. Nothing you'd want to keep secret, surely. Sometimes the note of Nate's voice might make you think he was pushing them in a certain direction but the guy who seemed to be in charge, who was sitting directly opposite him, was open to his suggestions and if the others had objections they didn't voice them very loudly.

There was even a jokey conversation about putting profits into overseas accounts. Letty thought her head may have jerked up to see how serious it was but Nate gave her a reassuring smile. They were just being light-hearted in an all-equals-together sort of way. She shouldn't take everything seriously.

'So if I hear you're having a trip to the

Isle of Man I'll know what you're up to,' Nate said.

'No, no, Bermuda,' the other man joked.

Nate gave a slow smile and nodded. 'Good call.'

She didn't think any of it was particularly amusing. But she wouldn't talk about it. Nate had made this easy for her. He deserved her loyalty. What did any of it mean, anyway?

There were three messages on Letty's phone when she next managed to look at it, what with the meeting, typing up her notes, and then catching up on other things that had mounted up while she was busy. Once she was in the local café, ready for lunch with Claire, she could finally look at them.

Her face must have betrayed some emotion when she saw they were all from Adam, but Claire was busy with her own phone and her sandwich and didn't ask.

The first one said, *Sorry didn't get back to you*.

The next one, only a minute later, was,

Can you do tonight?

He hadn't waited for her to reply before he suggested a time and place. The third message had been half an hour ago.

I should let him stew, was Letty's first thought. *Keep him waiting, just like he kept me waiting*.

Great, see you there, she typed. She pressed send, put her phone away and waited for Claire to finish her message so they could start to catch up. She was feeling a bit agitated and hoped Claire wouldn't notice.

'How was your weekend?' she asked.

'It was a bit disappointing actually,' Claire said. 'I'd arranged to see a friend on Saturday and it got cancelled.'

'Oh, no. Is this the same friend that cancelled on you the other day?'

'Ah, well, it sometimes happens.'

'You live on your own, don't you? At least if my arrangements fall through my flatmate is around at some point in the weekend.'

'Yes, well, it suits me to live alone.'

'Wasn't your sister around? You could

have gone to see her.'

'Yeah, I could have done that. But sometimes I've messed her around, telling her I was coming over and then having to cancel so I didn't want to risk doing that to her again. It's not nice.'

Letty sometimes thought Claire could be seeing a married man. She seemed to be constantly waiting for someone to be able to fit her in and anxious to keep her private life private, even from a flatmate. Maybe eventually she'd feel able to tell Letty about him.

'Her kids are OK, though?'

Claire's face softened. 'They're amazing. I adore them both.'

'Yes, they look like little sweethearts from that photo on your desk.' Letty always liked to look at that photo — Claire with her arms around two smiling little girls. Even if Claire's love life wasn't great she had family.

'I need to update that,' Claire said. 'They're ten and eleven now.' Claire's eyes clouded. Sad because she might not have her own children or sad they were growing up so fast, perhaps?

'I always think it would be awful to be without them,' she remarked.

'Why would you have to?' Letty asked. 'Your sister's not thinking of emigrating, is she?'

'No — nothing like that. Anyway, how about you? Good weekend?'

If Claire was keeping things from Letty, there were things she wasn't telling Claire either. Not yet. About Adam or the meeting. Well, there was nothing to tell about either. She glanced up.

'There's Terry at the counter — do you want to call him over?'

That would make sure Claire didn't ask awkward questions and she could get away with not discussing her weekend. Hoping to hear from Adam up to the last minute had spoiled her enjoyment of what she did.

Claire made space for him and Terry carried his sandwich and coffee over.

'Hi, Terry,' Letty said. 'How was your weekend?'

'It was chaotic, love.' He grinned and

took a bite of his sandwich.

'Aren't they all?' Claire said.

'How old are your kids?' Letty asked.

'The youngest is six and the oldest sixteen,' he said. 'But the sixteen-year-old, Rebecca, is disabled so everyone helps look after her.'

'That's nice.'

'So I don't know whose idea it was,' Terry went on. 'It was a couple of weeks ago but it took hold and between them they all decided we need a dog.'

Claire laughed. 'As if your house isn't full up enough already.'

'Right!' Terry agreed. 'I tried to insist it had to be a tiny one but Kate'—he looked at Letty—'my wife—quite rightly pointed out the risk of it getting trodden on.'

'That's true,' Claire said.

'So on Saturday we went to the rescue centre. Just to look, I told them, because the chances of them all agreeing were slim and I didn't want us to be arguing in front of the poor dogs.'

'No,' Letty agreed. You had to like

Terry. She was sure the children recognised that he cared for all of them — and he even cared for a load of dogs he'd never met, but which he knew probably had tough backgrounds like his kids.

'They were all drawn to this black part-Labrador, part who knows what else. He was a beauty but didn't come forward and beg for attention like some of the others so I tried to put them off. Not all dogs are going to want to be part of a boisterous family, I told them.

'Then — Midnight, his name was — over he comes, and puts his paw out to Rebecca. It was a job getting her wheelchair in and out between the pens, I tell you. So there's Midnight and Rebecca staring into one another's eyes and everyone went quiet and . . .'

'It was a done deal,' Claire suggested.

'It was, love. Before I knew it they'd come round to assess us, declared the house suitable and we could go and get him.' Terry had an extraordinary ability to eat while seeming to talk non-stop. 'The kids have drawn up a rota for walking and feeding. We live opposite the park so walking shouldn't be too much of a chore. They've put a line for cuddles and quiet time on the chart, too, and Rebecca's down to do that every day.'

'Aww.' Letty was certain she didn't want six children and a dog, but it was a very moving story. 'And your wife's happy?'

'Well, you know, her heart's broken for all the dogs we couldn't take home.' Terry wiped crumbs from his mouth and rubbed his hands together.

They all stood up and headed back to the office.

There was an older woman standing in the street outside the main door as they approached. She looked lost, but followed a group of workers from another company into the lobby, then stopped as they each swiped their cards to get through the barrier.

'Are you OK?' Letty asked.

'I thought there would be a reception desk where I could ask.'

'No, there's a line of bells outside,'

Terry told her. 'You ring up to the company you need and they'll come and collect you.'

'Oh. It's more than one company?'

'Ten or twelve of us, love. Who do you need?'

'I'm looking for my daughter.'

'And you don't know who she works for?' Now Claire was getting involved. She glanced at Terry when the woman just stood there helplessly.

'We can ask, can't we?' he said. 'If we knock at the doors of the other companies, it's only three or four each.'

Letty worried what Maria would have to say if she was very late back but the woman was quite distressed. You couldn't not help.

'What's your daughter's name?' she asked.

'Pamela Marr.'

'She's got your number, has she?' Letty asked. 'To give you a ring if she's not in.'

The woman shook her head sadly.

'I haven't seen her for nearly twenty

years.'

'Shall we take it, then, and pass it on if someone knows her?' Letty suggested.

'Tread carefully,' Terry advised as they parted to knock on the other companies' doors, armed with Pamela's mother's mobile number. 'If she's not been in touch for twenty years, there's a reason.'

* * *

As Letty expected, no one of that name was known in any of the offices. She was relieved. Sorry for the woman, of course, but she wasn't keen on being dragged into anyone's family history and this was clearly complicated. She was also pleased when Terry offered to go down and tell the woman they'd been unsuccessful, and she hurried to her desk.

Maria looked up, peering over the top of her unflattering square glasses at Letty and with what looked like disdain on her soft, round face. It looked as though she needed to go to the hairdresser's soon — her hair was looking lighter at the parting. Letty always wondered why she dyed it such a dark colour but they were never going to have a conversation where they discussed one another's style choices. Maria could easily find fault with Letty's long, blonde hair that hadn't seen a hairdresser's scissors for a year.

'I'm a bit late,' Letty explained. 'There was a woman downstairs looking for a long-lost daughter and some of us agreed to ask around.'

Maria was staring at her now without moving.

'Actually, you would know — has there ever been anyone working for this company called Pamela Marr?'

'What's this?' Nate came out of his room. He touched Maria lightly on the shoulder as she sat, still not moving. 'I just came out to ask you to come into my office for a moment,' he said, then turned to face Letty as she told her story.

He smiled and shook his head. It was a forced smile, it seemed to Letty. She supposed he had a lot on his mind and couldn't take on anyone else's problems.

Maria got up stiffly to go with Nate.

'Not a name I know,' Nate said, following her. 'No one of that name has ever worked for this company, have they, Maria?'

Maria turned at the door to his office, shook her head, and disappeared inside, followed by Nate. Well, she should have known Maria wouldn't have any sympathy for a woman seeking a long-lost daughter. Or any other human problem come to that.

* * *

Adam was at the bar when Letty arrived at the small pub they'd agreed on. There was an awkward moment when Letty wanted to pay for her own drink, but didn't manage to convince Adam and couldn't insist in case it became embarrassing. He looked so unhappy, she couldn't fight him.

They carried their drinks to a table in a corner and sat opposite one another. There was a short silence that Letty was reluctant to break because she was afraid they'd speak at the same time. Anyway, he needed to explain why he hadn't contacted her.

'Have you been to see your aunt?' she asked eventually, as Adam was taking a sip of his drink.

'Yes. There's no change.'

'Oh. That's a long time. So you still don't know any more?'

'No.' He hesitated. 'Letty, I'm sorry I didn't get in touch over the weekend.'

She waited for more. She wasn't going to say 'that's all right' — because it wasn't.

'All those questions you asked the neighbour,' Adam went on. 'It took me by surprise. I didn't want to think someone had hurt my aunt deliberately and it felt as if you were thinking that.'

'I didn't want her to have had a silly accident.'

'No.'

'I didn't really think it through any more than that. I don't know what I proved anyway by asking Eva all that.'

She took a sip of her own drink. 'What did they say at the hospital?'

'It wasn't a stroke or a heart attack,' Adam said. 'They've done all the tests they can, and a brain scan, and they can't see a reason why she might have blacked out.' He sighed. 'It's not that I wanted her to have heart problems or anything like that, Letty — this must sound terrible.'

'No.' Letty shook her head. 'You wanted a simple explanation — that's understandable.'

'I spent the whole weekend convincing myself you were wrong to look at other reasons. I suppose I wanted to kid myself for a bit longer and was afraid you'd sidetrack me from that comfort. But by Sunday when I went to the hospital, I knew something was wrong and your Miss Marple act was the way to go.'

He'd got in touch because he needed her problem-solving skills! So much for her romantic fancy.

Still, Letty had to smile at the 'Miss Marple act'. He'd lost the thoroughly miserable look he'd had and his eyes were twinkling at her again. There was still a chance they could be friends, or more, if she decided that was what she wanted as well. There was a fizzing inside her that indicated that was exactly what she wanted.

'What did you do at the weekend?' Adam asked. 'I hope you weren't hanging on waiting to hear from me.' He shook his head. 'If that doesn't sound too conceited.'

'I went out with my flatmate on Saturday,' she said, 'and to see my parents yesterday. That's always nice.'

'That's good.' Adam beamed. 'Do they live nearby?'

'Not too far.'

'And do you have any brothers or sisters?'

'No, it's just me. How about you? You're close to your aunt, but is there anyone else?'

'My parents went to live in rural France when I was a kid. They're still there but I came back as soon as I could.'

'Do you see them often?'

'A couple of times a year. Easy on the train.'

'So, no brothers or sisters either?'

He hesitated. 'I had an older brother. He died when I was about two.'

'How sad. I'm sorry to hear that, Adam.'

'That's one reason I stayed with them for so long. They were petrified something was going to happen to me as well.'

'Of course.'

'But I came here to university and sort of made a different life for myself. It would have been a bind, travelling every day to Paris for work from where they live.'

'What do you do?'

Adam hesitated. 'You're going to think it's not a job worth giving Paris up for.' He laughed. 'I did a degree in politics, and at the moment most of what I do is grant writing for charities.'

Letty's eyes widened. 'Is it? I used to work for a charity and if we'd known people like you existed, it might still be in operation today.'

The ice was well and truly broken as Adam talked about some of the organisations he'd helped and Letty told him how much she'd loved her previous job.

'What do you do now?'

'Admin in an accountancy company. It's not great, but the charity closed quickly once it folded and I had rent to pay.'

'Of course.'

'The guy I work for does all the IT and has some important clients of his own as well as managing the company. I might be able to get more involved somewhere along the line.'

Who was she kidding? She didn't even know she wanted to stay. But it sounded better than saying she was assistant to the assistant.

'That's good, that you've got possibilities.'

'I was just thinking about your family going to France. Miss Kemp didn't go with you, did she?'

Adam laughed. 'My aunt is far more

adventurous,' he said. 'She went around the same time to Argentina.'

'She's sometimes mentioned going abroad but I wasn't sure if it was just holidays. I thought she might have been to South America from some of the artwork on her walls and the little penguin-shaped jugs, but she never wants to talk about herself. How long was she there for?'

'Eighteen years, something like that.'

'Wow.'

'She lived in London for a while when she got back and then moved here.' Adam picked up his drink and looked into the glass thoughtfully. 'We were supposed to be looking after one another. I feel like I've let her down.'

Letty wondered whether to offer him another drink, though his glass was still half full, or if it was time to go. It didn't feel as though their relationship could go anywhere until Miss Kemp was better or Adam got over his guilty feelings.

'Oh, I forgot.' Adam felt in his pocket. He drew out a scrap of paper. 'I meant to show you this. The police found it on the floor near my aunt and wondered if she was trying to write a message.' He passed it to Letty. 'Is it shorthand?'

It was lined, as all shorthand paper is, probably torn from one of the notebooks Miss Kemp kept a supply of. The outlines were well formed. Letty pored over the lines and curves.

'That word's *thin*,' she said. '*Thin American* — but the 'n' isn't there, it says *America*. The next one could be threatening, then it's either *us* or *so* — *find* — something — *papers*. Then there's those numbers, *9599*.'

'*Thin American threatening so find papers*. Who can the thin American be?'

'I'm not a hundred per cent sure it's American. It could be *Moroccan* but it still hasn't got the 'n' at the end. Do you think your aunt knew many foreigners? Apart from Argentinians. It isn't that.'

'She knows a lot of people but I haven't heard her talk of a particular American or a Moroccan.'

Letty hesitated. She didn't want to

worry Adam even more.

'There was something I noticed, in your aunt's flat with you last Thursday. I just thought of it now with the mention of papers.'

'Go on.'

Adam held her gaze and Letty felt that disconcerting flutter. She had to look away to remember what she was going to say.

'You know how she has her books and files on the shelves behind her? They're always lined up and in order. If she gets one out, it goes back in the same place and she straightens them all up.'

Adam smiled. 'That sounds like my aunt.'

'I think some of the files might have dates on but you can't really see from where I sit. On Thursday I just felt there was something wrong. I wonder now if there was a file missing.'

Adam picked up his beer.

'I was going to offer you dinner, but . . .'

'No.' Letty drained her glass. 'Let's go

and look.'

At last there was something positive to do to try to solve the mystery of what had happened to Miss Kemp. And once that was solved, she could work out what might happen between her and Miss Kemp's attractive nephew.

4

'I feel a bit weird getting her private papers out,' Adam said, looking at the shelf of box files. 'It doesn't seem right.'

'I know what you mean, but if someone's threatening her and she's telling us to find the papers, we owe it to her to look.'

'I'm glad you're with me.'

That was strange. She couldn't make Adam out. One minute he seemed distant, the next she was certain he liked her. Like now, when he stood beside her giving her a long look. Letty had a feeling he was going to kiss her, but then he turned back to the files.

Why wasn't she daring enough to reach up and kiss him?

'They're in date order,' he said. 'Look, this last one's 2016 onwards.'

Letty shook off her disappointment about the kiss. She read too many romances. Truth to tell, she would be much better not to rush into this, regardless of her frustration at herself. If Adam was only interested in her as someone to have there while he found out about his aunt, that was as bad as her last boyfriend finding it convenient that she worked for the same company.

With a struggle Letty brought herself back to the moment.

'These must be the papers she meant,' she said. 'When was she in Argentina?'

'She left around the year 2000, or maybe a bit before that, and came back a year or two ago.'

'Maybe we should just start at the beginning and work our way through so we don't miss anything. Oh, two are missing — 1995 to '99 and 2000 to '04.'

The boxes seemed to contain bank statements, letters, household admin and other documents. The one marked 1985 to 1989 finished in December 1989, and the next one went from January 1990 to December 1994. The next two were missing, but the contents of the box marked *2005-2009* started at 1995.

'That's unlike your aunt, isn't it?' Letty said.

Adam nodded. 'She'd make sure the label was correct.'

'Unless she did that for a reason,' Letty said. 'Anyway, what do you think we're looking for?'

'No idea,' Adam said. 'I was sure this was the right thing to do, but it's going to take forever unless something leaps out at us.'

'I wonder if those numbers Miss Kemp wrote in the shorthand note, 9599, means 1995 to 1999,' Letty said after a while.

'That's one of the ones that is not here. At least, the papers are in a different one. What's going on?'

Letty put the box marked 2005 to 2009 down on the table.

'Did she change the labels to throw someone else off the scent?'

She walked round to her usual place. She didn't want to sit where Miss Kemp always sat.

'Let's start with that one, then, and

see if we're closer to knowing what we're looking for.'

Letty lifted the papers out and checked through quickly to see what they were up against. 'Shall we take a year each to start with?' she suggested, dividing them into piles. 'Oh — excuse me.' She laughed as her tummy rumbled loudly in the quiet room.

Adam laughed too. 'I was just wondering if Aunt Rowena would mind if we ordered a takeaway.'

'She'd never do it herself, but I don't think she'd want us to be hungry.'

'Indian or Chinese?' Adam asked. 'Or pizza?'

'Not pizza,' Letty said. 'We need to keep our hands clean!'

Now it felt comfortable again. Every now and then their eyes met and they shared a smile of understanding, or Letty glanced up and saw him deep in contemplation of his own pile of papers, a slight furrowing of his brow as he puzzled something out.

Her feelings would have to take a back

seat. The most important thing now was helping Rowena Kemp. She never doubted there was something of interest to be found. Her shorthand tutor wouldn't have sent her on a wild goose chase, and it looked as though she'd guessed there may come a time when she would need to preserve some of her documents.

* * *

When the food arrived, Adam went to get plates and she continued her careful look at the papers.

'What's this company, do you know?' she asked when he came back and they had dived in to the food. It was a company letterhead.

'Rawlings'? Yes, she worked there for years.'

'Why would she have this company bank statement?'

'Not sure. She was secretary to the boss so I suppose she would have access to the financial information. Why she would keep it is another question.' Adam studied the pages of figures. 'The ones that are highlighted are all going to the same place — it could be an offshore account.' He pointed to the recipient name. 'I'm pretty sure that's in the Cayman Islands.'

'They're large sums compared to the other transactions,' Letty reflected. 'Hundreds of thousands.' She put a hand to her mouth. 'Suppose she was storing it up to be a whistleblower?'

'Wow, that could have been dangerous. I wonder if that's why she's being threatened.'

'And here's a memo from the company director asking someone called Ethan to account for some missing money.'

They read the strongly worded memo together.

'There's a reference on it, DR/RK,' Letty said. 'Your aunt must have typed it.'

'But look what comes next.'

It was a cutting from an old local newspaper announcing the unexplained death of a well known businessman.

'*Derek Rawlings was popular in the neighbourhood for his generous donations to local charities*,' Adam read.

'There you are,' Letty interrupted. 'The DR from the memo — Miss Kemp's boss.'

'*Friends and family say they are shocked to learn his business was in trouble*,' Adam went on, reading from the cutting. '"*Derek managed to keep it hidden that we were losing so much money*,' said company accountant Ethan Marwick. '*It's tragic that he would take his own life over this.*"'

'Ethan Marwick — that's the name of the guy who received the memo, who they thought was siphoning off the funds.' Letty turned to take a forkful of food, well away from the papers. 'Is that how you say it, Marrick and not Marwick?'

'I suppose it could be either. How much does it matter, Letty?'

'No, I just wondered.' She hoped Adam wasn't getting tired of her querying everything. There were ideas struggling in her brain to come forward but remaining elusively wedged at the back. She had to question the details in case they turned out to be important but Adam seemed to be waiting for the big answer. 'I'm scared to look any further.'

'There's a later cutting about the business being wound up. Then —' Adam stopped short, holding up a photocopy of a photograph of a little boy who looked as though he was dressed for his first day at school. Some words were scrawled along the top.

'What does that say?' Letty said. 'That writing is almost as bad as my boss's.'

Adam was looking serious and Letty began to regret her frivolous remark. It was so easy to say the wrong thing.

'It says 'Cute little boy',' Adam said. 'But, Letty, that's me. My mum's got that same photo.'

'How old were you then?'

'Six or seven, I think.'

'You were seven in 1999?' Letty asked, surprised. 'You're twenty-eight?'

'Yes. How old are you?'

'Twenty-six. You look younger.'

'I've led a wholesome life.'

Letty laughed, despite the situation. When he relaxed, Adam was so easy to like. That made the reality unfolding even more scary.

'So this was a threat,' Letty said. 'Miss Kemp worked with this crook Ethan Marwick, however you say it.' She had gone with the pronunciation *Marrick*. 'She knew he was squirrelling company funds away offshore. He let her know he could harm you, and probably her as well, if she let on.'

'I wonder if that's why we all left the country.'

'Maybe she suspected he had a hand in the boss's suicide as well. Why would she keep those papers if not?'

There was a long silence. Letty's head was buzzing but she couldn't think straight any more.

Adam must have been feeling the same.

'Shall we call it a day?' he suggested.

'Yes, shall we? Suddenly I'm really

tired.'

They finished their food in silence. Then Letty tidied away the takeaway containers and Adam took plain paper from Miss Kemp's drawer, folded sheets around the pages they'd looked at and wrote *Seen* on them.

He had bold, neat handwriting, Letty noticed. To match his confident, straightforward manner.

He closed the files, looked at her and smiled.

'If I take these two home, we can meet at my flat next time and finish them. I could cook us something.'

Letty smiled back. She needed to stop imagining what this man was thinking of her. Even if it was purely to continue trying to find out what had happened to Miss Kemp, he didn't mind her coming to his home and he was willing to make her dinner.

And it would be more relaxed than being here.

She nodded. 'That sounds good.'

* * *

'How is the shorthand coming along?'

Maria didn't usually talk to Letty beyond telling her what to do next and making sure there was no detail pending, so this was an unusual question. She wondered if Maria was trying to be friendly or needed Letty to do more note-taking.

'I'm enjoying it. It's interesting.'

'Do you need more practice?'

'My teacher says it's too soon to go into real-life situations.'

'Does she? Is she any good, do you think? I mean, are you actually learning anything?'

'She's a brilliant teacher. I love her. How long did it take you to learn?'

Maria laughed without much amusement. 'I can't remember. It was a long time ago.'

'Did you learn in college?'

'Yes.'

It was on the tip of Letty's tongue to say there must have been more teachers in those days but she stopped herself for fear of Maria thinking she considered her to be very old.

What age must she be — mid-forties, getting on for fifty? A similar age to Nate probably, if they'd worked together for a long time. Even so, she would have been entering work at a time when shorthand was already considered old hat, surely.

'Do you want to go twice a week, or would that be too much? We could pay for an extra class.'

'I get homework in between.' Letty loved going to Miss Kemp's but two evenings a week for something with such limited use seemed excessive. Her social life hadn't really picked up yet but she still had hopes it would.

Maria nodded. 'OK.' She was looking at Letty. Perhaps she understood Letty had a life outside of work.

'Besides, my tutor's in hospital at the moment.'

Maria looked shocked. 'Really? In hospital?'

'She had an accident.'

'An accident?'

What was wrong with her colleague, repeating everything she said? It was unlike Maria to be incoherent. She'd been odd over Letty asking about Pamela Marr as well.

'She's called Miss Kemp. Do you know her?' she asked. All Letty knew was that once she'd agreed to the lessons, someone in the office organised it all for her. Miss Kemp didn't seem to know Maria but Letty could have misunderstood that. 'I'm sorry, should I have mentioned it before? She's in intensive care so you can't visit at the moment.'

Maria seemed to shake herself. 'No. I don't know her. Well, I'm sorry to hear that, Letty. Do keep me informed of the situation.'

'I will.' Perhaps Maria was worried this would delay Letty's progress. 'And I'll carry on the chapters in the book we're using so I don't stop learning.'

'Yes,' Maria said vaguely. She turned and hurried over to Nate's door, knocked and disappeared inside.

Why was Maria making such a fuss? Letty almost wished she hadn't agreed to the classes.

Except then she wouldn't have met Miss Kemp.

Or Adam.

* * *

Letty loved living close to the park. You could walk into town along its gravel paths and under a canopy of leaves. It was especially gorgeous in autumn when the trees showed different shades of red and yellow, but it was lovely earlier in the year too, when it was light until late. She liked the way the sun dappled through the branches in the daytime and how later the shadows of the trees lengthened. It was interesting how you breathed more deeply away from the streets and traffic, and how your shoulders dropped and tension lifted.

And now it looked as though she could walk across the park and then on to Adam's in less than fifteen minutes.

Close enough to be really convenient . . . but far enough away for there not to be a risk of always bumping into him if, once all this was over, it didn't work out between them.

Once all this was over. She needed to stop thinking of Miss Kemp's situation as something to be got over so she could get on with her life. This was really serious. It was just that it seemed unbelievable that something like this would happen to someone she knew.

'Ahoy, there,' a voice called from behind and she turned to see a man pushing a wheelchair. As Letty turned and called a greeting, a black dog leaped on to the lap of the girl in the chair and she squealed with delight.

'Midnight!' Terry admonished. 'This is Letty who I work with. She's not going to do any harm to your beloved mistress.'

'Who's taking who for a walk?' Letty asked, grinning.

The dog watched her warily. 'He's so protective of Rebecca,' Terry said. He looked pleased.

'Good to meet you, Rebecca,' Letty said and the girl continued smiling. 'Have all the others given up on the dog walking rota already?'

'Not at all. This is going to be the fittest, most walked dog in the district. We just had to go to the chemist and Midnight wanted to come with us.'

'Coming along for the ride, eh?'

Rebecca didn't answer but seemed very happy to have the dog on her lap.

'He's beautiful,' Letty added. She hoped that another day she'd be allowed to touch his shiny black head and ruffle those big floppy ears, but it clearly wasn't going to be today.

As Terry took the path to their right and Letty continued straight, she noticed the dog jumped down.

What a lovely relationship that was going to be.

* * *

Adam led her into his open-plan kitchen diner and living room.

'This is a nice room.' She handed Adam a bottle of winet. 'Are all the books yours?'

'Some are my flatmate's. He's away travelling.'

'Lucky for him. Where is he heading for?'

'He's probably in Vietnam at the moment.'

'Brilliant.'

'Sit down.' Adam gestured towards the sofa. 'I'll pour us some wine.' He got out two glasses, then peered into a bubbling pot. 'I should warn you that I can't actually cook.'

'That's all right — neither can I.' She laughed. 'Something smells nice, though.'

'It's sauce out of a jar.' He handed her a glass of wine and sat on the sofa.

'What other sort is there?'

That set the tone for their conversation throughout the meal, laughing and light-hearted.

'How do you become a grant writer?' Letty asked.

'That you pick up as you go along,' Adam said. 'I didn't mean to mislead. I actually run a business services company and we try to provide more modestly priced services to charities. You'll have seen from your work that getting the grant approvals in is crucial and they're so time-consuming, it makes sense sometimes to outsource them.'

'I can see that, but back-track a bit — you run the company?'

'Does that sound like boasting? It's tiny.'

'Not boasting but now I'm confused.'

'Look, a couple of years after we left uni a group of us got together and realised that none of us were majorly happy with the jobs we'd got. We got a bit drunk and started fantasising. We worked out that between us we had a full set of skills to establish a company that could provide small businesses with services like accountancy, graphic design, legal advice, stuff like that.'

'Great. So what else do you do?'

'All sorts. Copywriting, marketing,

translations sometimes. And I'm sort of the general manager, I suppose.'

'Do you have an office?' Letty looked around the flat. 'You don't work here?'

'We rent a little office space in town. There are only two of us who work full-time so we save on rent and it usually works out that not everyone wants to be in the office at the same time.' He laughed. 'And the legal adviser is doing pretty well in her practice so we have our monthly meetings in her house — it's massive.'

'It sounds like you all get on well together.'

'We're really lucky.'

'I wish I'd gone to something more useful like computer programming classes rather than shorthand so I could join you.' As soon as the words were out she regretted them, but Adam smiled.

'Sorry to say that's already covered. The other full-time person I work with, Sam, is a computer expert.'

'Dang.' Letty laughed.

'But when you get your certificates we

can advertise shorthand note-taking if you like.'

Of course, it was a professional business. Even if it was Adam's company, they wouldn't take anyone on without qualifications.

'Thank you. What do you think, might there be one taker every five years or so?'

That was an odd thought. In other times Letty might have been tempted into the 'where do you want to be in five years' time?' conversation but now she felt adrift, with no ideas.

She didn't want to be where she was now, that was for sure — certainly not in her current job. Nor still learning shorthand. On the other hand, 'in a secure relationship' might well be on her list.

And for the first time in months, she began to think that might be possible. His hand brushed hers as he poured her more wine. She felt herself flush and hoped he wouldn't notice, but he was looking away from her. Was he oblivious? Did he not mean it to happen? Or did he mean it to happen and it affected him as well?

It wasn't until the plates were cleared away that both their minds turned to the mystery that had brought them together, and Adam brought out the two box files. They worked hard for more than an hour, checking page after page in both of them, then sat back for a moment to take stock. For a moment Letty had almost forgotten where she was, and who she was with, as she'd entered Miss Kemp's world and tried to imagine why each piece of information was there.

When the last page was turned over and Adam and Letty looked at one another, it was hard for Letty to concentrate for a moment as her insides fizzed when she met his eyes.

'Right, what do we know?' Letty fussed with her notebook as Adam closed the two box files. It didn't look as though they'd extracted much information, especially as there had been very little of any use after the year 2000. A dozen relevant pages sat in a folder Adam had found.

'We know Rowena worked in the same company as someone called Ethan Marwick in the 1990s,' Adam began. Letty noticed he was pronouncing it *Marrick* now. 'The head of the company, Derek Rawlings, got into financial difficulties and apparently died or took his own life in 1999.'

Letty took up the story. 'Rowena had been Derek's secretary and had typed a memo from Derek asking for an explanation of some company funds that had gone missing. She kept or later got hold of the relevant bank statements, but there's no evidence the police were involved or that the money was repaid.'

'Yes,' Adam said. 'Then, also in 1999, Rowena received threats against her family.'

'Are we making too much of it to say the threats must have come from the person defrauding the company who found out she suspected them?'

'I would tend to think not because it's in the same box with that information, and my aunt is very orderly.'

Letty nodded. 'And we think it's this Ethan Marwick who did the fraud and the threatening.'

'Yes.'

Adam watched as Letty added to her notes. She'd moved from longhand to shorthand to get everything down, but suddenly she stopped writing and looked stricken.

'Letty, what's the matter? You don't look well.'

Letty felt a rush of blood to her head and couldn't speak for a minute.

'It's not *a thin American*, Adam,' she said shakily. 'From the note Miss Kemp left last week.' The two words were phonetically similar but she'd missed the mark for capital letters on the word she'd thought was *thin*. Miss Kemp didn't always do them clearly. 'It's *Ethan Marwick* threatening her.'

5

Neither Maria nor Nate were at their desks when Letty arrived the next morning, and she hoped she might get away without talking much to anyone that day.

She would meet Adam again in the evening. There was no point thinking round and round in circles about what they'd discovered. There was still so much more to find out — but it didn't stop her thinking about it.

Letty had a rule never to do any personal internet searching at work. It could get compulsive and before you knew where you were, an hour could have gone by and you were further from your original goal than ever. It wouldn't be right to do that in work time. Especially not knowing who might be looking over your shoulder.

It hadn't taken long the evening before to look up the name Ethan Marwick, sitting up in bed with her laptop. It must be an unusual name. Unless he was a schoolboy in Slough or an ice hockey player, there was no sign of him online.

Just to satisfy herself she also looked for Pamela Marr. That was a different case — there were so many, she didn't know how to narrow it down. Pamela had to be at the very least thirty, given the probable age of her mother, and at most fifty, and she could live anywhere, be anything.

For a moment Letty wondered about disappearing from everyone who knew you and starting a new life. She wouldn't do it to her parents, that was for sure, but she could see how for some people it might be exhilarating to start afresh. Maybe Pamela Marr had done that.

So all in all, it had been a difficult night once she tried to sleep, and Letty still felt out of sorts this morning. She plodded on with some work that didn't require much thought.

Maria didn't appear until nearly mid-day, hurrying and looking unusually dishevelled. Letty glanced round to say hello and was surprised at what she saw. It looked as though her work colleague had got up late and not had time to blow-dry her usually tidy short dark hair. She nodded towards Letty and while Letty was still swivelled round greeting her, Maria got her mirror out to try to tease her hair back into shape.

Letty smiled to herself, feeling guilty to be pleased to see her colleague having a bad hair day for once — but not too guilty.

* * *

'I've just come from the hospital,' Adam said as he met Letty inside Miss Kemp's building that evening. They'd decided to look at the rest of the files and decide what to do. There was a slim chance there could be something else of interest among Miss Kemp's papers. There were such a lot of question marks remaining over this mystery, that Letty in particular felt a need to have all the available information.

It meant it wouldn't be right to prioritise their personal life — if indeed Adam was even thinking the way she was. Sometimes she thought he wasn't but often, when he looked at her or they laughed together, she was certain he was.

'I spoke to her,' Adam said, sounding pleased. 'She's been transferred to a ward and was sitting up in bed looking fine.'

'Oh, I'm so glad.'

'But she can't remember anything about what happened. She felt OK and didn't understand why she was in hospital.'

'Did you speak to the doctor?'

'That's the problem. Now it feels wrong to talk about her without Rowena being present too. She said they're running more tests and she'll let me know when the results come in, but she's ready to go home the minute they let her.'

'We need to find out what's going on before that happens,' Letty said. 'Or can you think of somewhere else she could go, where she'd be safe?'

‘I suggested she came to stay with me, but she wasn’t impressed with the idea.’

The lift arrived and they got in.

‘Is there anyone else you can think of whose house we could convince her to go to? Do you have any more aunts or uncles? Or cousins?’

‘It’s just her and my dad. She might go there, I suppose, assuming she’s well enough to travel. If we can persuade her it’s too dangerous to stay here.’

‘She’s your dad’s sister? But you’ve got a different surname.’

‘Yeah, they changed it for me in France when we first got there. It was never clear why, but it helped with some document or another. I didn’t argue the toss too much. It meant a lot to them so I didn’t make a fuss and haven’t thought to ask about it since. Maybe I will, next time I go.’

Adam put the key in the lock and Letty followed him in to Miss Kemp’s living room. It all felt the way it always did, the pot of pencils in the middle of the desk where she’d replaced it on Monday.

'Maybe it was to keep you safe,' Letty suggested.

Adam stopped with the key in his hand and Letty felt a rush of sympathy for him. This must all be hard to cope with. He was only now beginning to understand why his life had changed so dramatically when he was a child, and why his parents worried about him.

'Yeah — perhaps I won't mention it . . .' Then Adam stopped short and she followed his gaze, across the room.

The part of the shelf that had contained the box files of papers was empty. Someone had taken the other documents they wanted to look at.

The books that had stood either side of the files were lined up neatly, where they always were, slightly tilted to stand up straight now there was nothing on the other side to keep them upright.

Feeling very uncomfortable, they searched the rest of the flat, not sure what they were looking for, and not knowing if a space meant something was missing. Nothing obvious came to light.

‘I wish we’d gone through the rest of the files while we had the chance,’ Adam lamented. ‘We have no idea if there’s anything interesting in the rest.’

‘Well, at least we have those two safe.’

‘I suppose so. And at least we weren’t here when whoever it was came for them.’

Letty shuddered. ‘How did they get in?’

They checked the doors and windows. No sign of a forced entry.

Letty was reluctant to suggest another chat with Eva, because it was there her hopes for a growing relationship with Adam seemed to be nipped in the bud and she didn’t want to alienate him further with her ‘Miss Marple act’. But in case there was the slightest chance Eva could have seen anything, they needed to ask.

‘I might just check with Eva whether she heard anyone go in,’ she said tentatively. ‘Do you want to stay here — or go and I’ll text you if anything comes of it?’

‘No — good idea. I’ll come with you.’

That was good. They were on the same page after all.

Adam let her out through the front door, checked he had the keys and then pulled it to. She waited beside him. It was only a few steps over to Eva's door but she didn't want to look too eager.

Well, to be honest, she wasn't that eager. It was scary to think someone had got into Miss Kemp's private space twice without leaving a clue as to who they could be or how they got in. And she didn't want to make the nice neighbour worried about her own safety.

Adam seemed to hesitate a moment as well. She thought he was reluctant to have to think about the danger to his aunt. His arm brushed hers as he slipped the keys into his pocket. She stood still and turned to look up at him. His eyes met hers and the air between them felt electric. Then Adam gently put one arm around Letty's shoulders and drew her closer. He had to bend to place a gentle kiss on her lips. She tilted her face up to kiss him properly as her arms went around his back and his other arm came around her.

So she hadn't misunderstood the tension between them . . .

They were both a little breathless when they broke apart, and Adam looked into her eyes for a long moment.

She was glad he didn't say anything. Sometimes a look was more truthful.

He gently pulled her head to his chest and they stood there, Letty feeling Adam's heartbeat, Adam stroking her hair, until they both sighed and took those steps across the hallway back to reality.

Adam let her do the talking to start with, and Eva asked them in.

'Yes — didn't you know?' Eva looked at Adam as they sat down. 'Rowena asked your sister-in-law to pick some things up for her. I spoke to her as she was going in yesterday.'

Letty felt Adam jump beside her.

'Sister-in-law?' he repeated and Eva nodded.

'Do you know what things?' Letty

asked. 'Did you see her going out again?'

'No. I assumed it was nightwear and the like, toiletries maybe, for the hospital. I was surprised, to be honest, because Rowena had never spoken about your brother having married or ever seeing his wife. I'm afraid I didn't understand the story of your brother at all as I thought Rowena told me he'd died as a child. I'm sorry if it's all more recent than I thought.'

'What did she look like, the woman?' Letty asked.

Eva glanced at Adam again. 'Oh, don't you know her? She was, I don't know, a couple of inches taller than me. I'm five foot two. Not slim, and around forty-five or fifty. I was surprised she'd be that age. I didn't know your brother was that much older than you.' She hesitated as if confused. 'Or maybe he married an older woman, I don't know, it's not for me to judge.'

'That's all right,' Letty said gently. 'What colour hair?'

'That's another odd thing,' Eva said. 'It was blonde but I'm fairly sure it was a wig. It wasn't at all a nice healthy blonde like yours.' She nodded over to Letty, who reached round to finger the uneven ends half way down her back. 'It didn't suit her at all,' Eva went on. 'But she had a door key that Rowena must have given her so I couldn't stop her going in.'

'Of course not.' Letty hesitated. 'If we give you Adam's mobile number, would you get in touch if anyone else comes to the flat?'

'Yes, of course, but you know it's only chance if I see them, don't you? Once I'm in my flat I don't hear what's going on out there.'

Adam nodded. 'Just in case, though.'

It was the first time he'd spoken since the shock of the fake sister-in-law.

They didn't exchange a word as they left Eva's flat and walked across to Miss Kemp's. Letty saw Adam examine the lock as they went in, as if it could answer the question of who had opened it before them.

'You can't disbelieve her, can you?' he said.

Letty shook her head. 'I don't think she'd make all that up. I mean, why would she?'

'Do you think she's particularly forgetful?' Adam hovered at the open door to the room with the missing files.

'Could we sit in the kitchen?' Letty said. 'I don't want to have to look at that empty shelf.'

'Sure.'

The table in the kitchen was small and pushed against one wall. It meant sitting much closer to Adam, with their knees almost touching.

But this wasn't at all the moment to reflect on being close to Adam Taylor, however disturbing — delightfully disturbing — it was.

Instead, Letty thought about his question.

'Forgetful?' she repeated. 'No, I don't think so. On the contrary, she seems very on the ball.'

'That's what I thought. I was thinking about the story of her not finding Aunt Rowena's key and not remembering when it went missing.'

'I thought that sounded very possible,' Letty said. 'I could do that myself.'

'Sure, but coming just after the story of the plumbers, it got me thinking.'

'And?'

'I didn't like the sound of how they got into her flat and I know you didn't either. When I saw you getting so suspicious — well, later when I thought about it, really — it made me wonder whether they took her spare keys.'

'Yes!' It was possible. 'But, Adam, the blonde woman — could it be someone from your family?'

'There's literally no one it could be. Someone from the hospital, maybe, but why would they tell the story of being Rowena's niece-in-law?'

'No.'

'And, Letty, I don't want to sound self-important, but she'd ask me. I know it might be personal things, and for all I know she might have got me to take a woman friend to help, like with the toiletries, but she wouldn't give a key to random people with wigs.' He laughed. 'Even if she didn't have the wig on at the time.'

Letty tended to agree. She was side-tracked by the question of who Adam would take to help him but he was a great guy. He'd have a lot of friends.

'I know what you mean,' was all she said.

'Oh,' Adam said, as if remembering something else. 'I did a search for our Ethan Marwick and there's no contemporary entries for him on the internet. At least, no one who can be our guy.'

'No, I did that too.'

'Unless he's a basketball player.'

Letty laughed. 'Or hockey.'

'And nothing about the company he was involved in before,' Adam added.

'It's odd, isn't it? It's hard not to have a trace on the internet.'

'Unless you wiped it.'

'Can you do that?' Letty asked.

Adam shook his head. 'If you know what you're doing, maybe. I'll ask Sam in my office. You could ask your boss at work as well if it can be done that thoroughly.'

Letty hesitated for a long time. 'I could.'

She probably wouldn't, though, and she wasn't sure why.

'Would it be all right if I went to see your aunt tomorrow?' Letty asked. 'She may have remembered something else and maybe I can tell her about the note she wrote in shorthand, in case that jogs her memory.'

'Yes, do.' He hesitated. 'Just don't be too disappointed if she doesn't know what you're talking about.'

'I promise not to push her if she doesn't,' Letty said. She stood up, knowing that whatever happened the next day at the hospital, there would be a reason to see Adam again.

He approached her as they stood on the street and gave her a friendly kiss on the cheek. She responded with a kiss of her own and smelled something like coconut on his skin or hair. Then they turned to go their separate ways.

Letty wondered if Adam was thinking about what might happen if they were to hold one another close again. Her heart beat faster at the idea and she hoped his was doing the same.

6

Letty trudged along corridors and up staircases. Why did they all look the same in hospitals and seem so endless? This hospital did at least signpost everything, and Letty finally reached the ward she was headed for, got buzzed in and sanitised her hands.

'I'm looking for Rowena Kemp, please,' she asked a passing nurse.

'Oh, ask at the desk.'

There was a lot going on at the desk and it was a good few minutes before anyone could hear her repeat who she was looking for, during which time Letty had a look at the list of patients on the wall and at some labels on doors and began to think Miss Kemp had been moved. That was fine, there was an hour of visiting time left, assuming all wards kept the same timetable.

'Rowena left earlier today — didn't anyone tell you?' the busy nurse at the desk said.

'Left?'

'She was discharged.'

'Ah, no, I didn't know.' That was a surprise.

'Or she discharged herself, I'm not sure how it worked out in the end.'

'Did her nephew come to take her home?'

Letty was sorry Adam hadn't thought to tell her, but it must have been a surprise to him as well that his aunt was fit to go home so soon.

'No. Just a minute, I'll find out.' The nurse turned and made a phone call.

Eventually it transpired that there had been something left at the reception desk. The nurse hung up and looked in several muddled trays of papers. Eventually she unearthed an envelope.

'What's your name?'

'Letty Wood.'

'The nephew's Adam, isn't he? I've met him.'

'Yes.'

'She left this for you.'

Letty took the envelope, murmured her thanks and wandered away.

Adam & Letty was written on the sealed envelope.

Before she left the ward she had second thoughts and went back to the nursing staff work station.

'Is there anyone who would be able to describe the person Rowena Kemp went with earlier?' When the nurse looked reluctant to engage further she added, 'There has been confusion in the family before over who does what.'

It sounded lame but after the incident with the files going missing on the day an unknown woman had been into Miss Kemp's flat, Letty wanted to give Adam as much information as she could. She held her breath, wondering if they were going to describe the same woman to her now.

Fortunately a young man in a darker blue uniform checking a screen on the shelf looked up and winked. 'No mistaking the looker Rowena Kemp walked out with this morning,' he said. 'Tall, slim, walks like a dancer — does that ring any bells?'

'No, but I can tell her nephew. She was happy to go with him, was she?'

'Darling, I tell you, half the patients wanted to go with him as well.' He laughed. 'And some of the staff too.'

That didn't really answer the question, but it gave her something to tell Adam. She hoped that it wasn't the mystery she was making of it.

She walked quickly downstairs, found somewhere to sit and opened the letter.

There were just seven shorthand outlines. The last two Letty thought were Miss Kemp's signature. That was interesting; she'd elided the *w* and written the sign for a diphthong for the two vowel sounds in her first name. But the trademark tiny mark for capitals was there, and the last word of the message had that mark as well and could definitely be *Kemp*.

I am safe with — and then a name. Not *Frederic* because the first curve would be doubled. Not Patrick because it would start with a straight line and be higher up, above the ruled line.

Perhaps it was a short form she hadn't learned yet. No — a name wouldn't be a short form, would it? Unless you made your own up.

Letty got out her phone.

'Adam, where are you?'

'Letty, I didn't expect to hear from you so soon. Didn't you go to see Aunt Rowena?'

'Are you at home?'

'No. Do you want me to come and meet you? Where are you?'

'I'm still in the hospital.'

'So you did see her? What's wrong?'

She hadn't wanted to tell him on the phone and now she was making it worse.

'Listen,' he said. 'Come out of the main entrance, cross over and turn left. There's a pub. I'll meet you inside. Ten minutes.'

* * *

It was a busy pub. Letty hovered in the doorway for a while hoping to see Adam, and he came in just a minute after her. She could have hugged him with relief, but concern was written on his face. He guided her to a space where they could talk and looked at her questioningly.

'I went to the hospital and they said your aunt had been discharged, or discharged herself, it wasn't clear. She left, anyway — but there was a letter for us.'

She handed the envelope to him. He opened it quickly, looked at the contents and gave her another questioning look.

'It says '*I am safe with*' and then I can't read the name, and that's her name at the end. I went back to the ward to ask who she'd left with and they told me it was a tall, slim, good-looking man who walked like a dancer.'

'What does the name look like?'

'It looks like Frederick but it's not that.'

Adam nodded. 'Ah. Federico.'

Letty frowned. 'Yes, it could be that.' She wouldn't have written the name like that. She definitely needed to ask Miss Kemp how to do names in shorthand.

'Who's Federico?' she asked.

'Shall we have a drink?' Adam suggested.

She nodded and made for the bar. 'My turn.'

By the time she returned, Adam had cleared a table for them and he jumped up to help her.

'So, who's Federico?'

Adam took a sip of his beer. 'When I was about thirteen, I suppose, my aunt came over to visit us in France one Christmas and New Year. She'd found a house to rent in the next village and brought a male friend with her. They'd let me have a friend to stay so I didn't have much to do with them, I'm ashamed to say. You know what thirteen-year-olds are like.'

Letty nodded, smiling. 'I used to be one.'

'I do remember my parents often talking about this guy, Fede, afterwards when my aunt was mentioned.'

'She hasn't talked to you about him

since she's been back?'

'No, and I'm sorry to say I didn't ask. And my dad knows I see her and hasn't said anything either. I suppose I assumed they weren't together any more.'

Letty was busy revising her view of Miss Kemp.

'So they were — together?'

'I didn't give it any thought at the time, but I reckon they were.' He paused. 'It's a cliché but they did the tango together and even two teenage boys recognised it was something special. They tried to teach my mum and dad and they laughed about how bad they were and how very good Rowena and Fede were.'

Miss Kemp doing the tango with a sexy Latino . . . Then Letty started to remember something else.

'When we were talking to the neighbour that first time, she talked about your aunt going away sometimes. Do you know who she would stay with?'

'Well, she had a couple of friends she always kept in touch with. I suppose if I thought anything, I imagined it was either of them.' He put his glass down and turned to Letty. 'Don't think badly of me, Letty. My aunt has a way of shifting the conversation away from personal talk. I would have said we were close — but I know really little about her life.'

'I can imagine. I know it's different with a student-tutor relationship but I asked the other day how long she'd been in that flat and was really surprised it was only five or six months. I imagined she'd been there for ever but there was no way to ask any more questions.'

'No. I never got to the bottom of why she came back — and you're right, it was only a matter of months ago — but my dad hasn't been able to find out either. I'm pretty sure he doesn't know Fede's here either.'

'Did you tell your parents about Miss Kemp's accid — about her being in hospital?'

Adam shook his head. 'I didn't see the point in worrying them.'

'No.'

There was a long silence between them, then Adam gave a half-smile.

'So now what do we do?'

That was good. Adam didn't want to let this go either. Miss Kemp had been attacked and papers taken which should have related to some accusations of fraud more than twenty years ago. It was only apparent misfiling on Miss Kemp's part that meant Adam had the relevant files. No; Miss Kemp had surely deliberately put the wrong dates on her files to put anyone else off the scent. Now she had disappeared, and they couldn't get in touch.

'I'd like to know where this Argentinian lives and see if there's a way of making sure your aunt really is OK,' she said.

'I wondered about that as well.' He sighed. 'I hate secrecy. I really wish we could sit down and talk openly. But I don't mean forcing Aunt Rowena to talk about personal stuff if she doesn't want to.' He looked at Letty. 'Well, you know what I mean.'

She smiled. She did know what he

meant and she loved it that he expected her to understand. And that he'd understood that she needed to see him when she called from the hospital. She wondered how far she could push this.

'Do you think your aunt has anything like an address book where we might find Federico's address?'

'What — do we search her flat again?'

Put like that, it didn't sound like a good suggestion. Letty didn't answer. She finished her drink and put the glass down. This was the moment for Adam to suggest another one . . . or for them each to go home.

'I suppose we could,' he said eventually.

He drained his own glass and stood up.

* * *

They'd been through the drawers and cupboards in Miss Kemp's office on their previous visit, but couldn't be sure they'd not overlooked an address book as that hadn't been what they were looking for. So they looked again.

They went into the kitchen next, though it didn't seem likely they'd find it there. It was to delay going into the bedroom, Letty thought; that seemed too intrusive. But as a ruse it didn't delay them for long.

There was a wardrobe, a dressing table, some shelves and two bedside cabinets with drawers. The paintings on the walls were small but in vibrant colours, including one that consisted of coloured horizontal lines covering the canvas that immediately made Letty think of a sunset.

She tore her eyes away to get on with the task in hand, amazed at the way you can imagine such a thing from just lines and colours. She wondered if she would ever have a conversation with Rowena Kemp about the pictures in her bedroom and whether she'd find out if it was indeed called *Sunset*. She thought not.

Tentatively, and not sure she would have Miss Kemp's blessing to do this,

Letty tried the drawers on one of the pieces of furniture on either side of the bed — not the one with the books on the top which was probably the one Miss Kemp made most use of. Delaying tactics again, she knew.

She glanced across to the other side. Was that the latest Marian Keyes on the top of the pile? So Miss Kemp was going to think about translating it into shorthand. How amazing.

'She probably keeps all contacts on her phone,' she said, moving over to that side. Miss Kent was a modern woman.

But she didn't hear Adam's response because she opened the other drawer and froze in shock.

She slammed it quickly shut, backing away from the piece of furniture.

'Letty — what?' Adam was by her side within seconds.

She couldn't speak. She watched him gingerly open the drawer and meet her eyes.

'Why on earth has Aunt Rowena got a gun in her bedside cabinet?'

'And why didn't she use it on her intruder?'

'Letty!' Adam laughed. 'I'm surprised at you.'

Once over her initial shock, Letty approached the drawer again. Adam held up his hand.

'This may be a totally ridiculous thing to say but don't touch it.'

She laughed as well, wondering if they may both be a little hysterical. 'You've been watching too many forensic detective shows.'

But she didn't mind giving the little gun a wide berth. She eased out an A5-sized book with a firm plastic cover, letting the pistol slide off the top.

Seeing it, Adam gasped. 'So is that it?'

She nodded and handed it to him. 'Do you think we could have a cup of coffee?'

Back in the kitchen, Letty made coffee while Adam leafed through the address book.

'Do you know this guy's surname?' she asked.

'No — but here's one of the old friends.

I recognise her name. She lives in Deal and I seem to recall the other one is on the coast as well. Oh, yes — here. Isle of Wight.'

Letty put the mugs on the table and Adam passed her the book. He looked uncomfortable.

Had she been wrong to encourage him to do this? If it was against his principles? If he felt this bad just finding the address, how was he going to feel staking out his aunt wherever she was staying? They were in too far now to turn back.

Letty couldn't pretend she hadn't found the right entry — she physically jumped as she saw it.

'Have you found him?'

Adam sounded wary. She needed to give him the chance to back off.

'Yes, this is him. Federico Maldonado.' She caught Adam's eye. 'No phone number — but there's an address in London.'

Adam put his mug down carefully and aligned it with the edge of the table, then pushed it back.

'Fancy a trip to London?'

* * *

Maria was closeted with Nate when Letty arrived at work the next morning, and when she came out, she asked Letty to go in.

The boss went over a few things Letty was engaged in, for no good reason that she could see except to let her know he was in charge.

She knew that. It was a pity he couldn't see after all these weeks that he could leave something in her hands and trust her to do it well.

The phone rang while Nate was speaking and Letty half rose to go.

'Stay,' he said, and she had to listen to one side of a conversation that appeared to have no real content but still went on and on.

She looked surreptitiously at her watch. Surely she wasn't going to have to waste three-quarters of an hour on all this?

She was.

'Sorry about that,' Nate said when the call ended. 'Just recap for me,' and she had to repeat her progress update. She hoped all this wouldn't mean she couldn't leave on time — she had preparations for her trip to make this evening.

'I've booked the train and a small hotel,' Adam had called to tell her, and they arranged what time to meet and at which station.

At lunchtime she walked down to see Claire.

'I haven't much time today, but are you going to the café for lunch? I'll sit in if you are — otherwise I'll just bring something back to my desk.'

'OK, I'll go.' Claire looked pleased. 'Terry's running some errands and I didn't fancy eating on my own.'

'Why haven't you got much time?' Claire asked as they headed out. 'Anything going on up your end of the office?'

'I don't think so. Nate seemed a bit distracted this morning and everything took longer than it needed to.'

Claire smiled. Perhaps she was pleased to know even Nate got distracted sometimes.

'How's Maria these days?' Claire asked.

'As ever,' Letty said. There wasn't anything to report. 'I notice you never come up to see me when she's there — or when he is, come to that.'

Claire touched Letty on the back of the shoulder as they went into the little lunch place. 'Don't want to get you into any trouble,' she said. 'And if Maria's there, even if it's work we're talking about there's always that sense she's straining to hear.'

'I don't think Nate minds me having a couple of minutes' break to chat every now and then.' Letty laughed. 'Though Maria probably does.'

'Exactly.'

There was a pause in the conversation as they ordered and found a table, and Letty tried to get in first before Claire could. 'So, have you got anything planned for the weekend?' she asked. She was probably asking for the question to be turned back on her.

'I'm meeting a friend and we're going

shopping,' Claire said.

'Nice. Anything particular you're looking for?'

'I need a whole new wardrobe, basically. I haven't bought any new clothes for years, it seems like. I feel like a different look.'

'And why not?' Letty picked up on Claire's enthusiasm and was glad for her. Maybe things were going well with her man. 'I had to reinvent myself a bit when I got this job — I'd always gone to work in jeans and T-shirts. I'm happiest back in the jeans when I'm out of the office, though.'

'That's a good way of putting it, reinventing yourself. Maybe I'll do that.'

'Don't scare your nieces by being too different. They'll wonder where their Aunty Claire has gone.'

Letty was still making light of it but Claire's eyes seemed to cloud over and the laughter went from them. She hoped she hadn't made Claire sad again and hoped her sister wasn't planning on moving away so she'd see less of them.

'Have you been to the new shop in the high street?' Letty went on hurriedly. 'I had a look in the window and they have some really interesting things in there.'

'Yes, I had a look too and wouldn't mind going in tomorrow. It's nice to find something a bit different to what's in all the other shops.'

'I'll look forward to finding out what you think.'

'So, what are you up to this weekend?' Claire asked.

Letty wasn't sure why she was so keen on Claire not knowing what she was doing. Claire wasn't a gossip, and never pressed her further than she was comfortable with. She definitely didn't want to rub it in that she had a boyfriend she went away for weekends with, if it was true Claire's boyfriend was married and they could never do that.

Except Letty wasn't even sure Adam was a boyfriend . . .

'I'm going to my parents',' she said, mentally crossing her fingers behind her back. Claire and she never met at the weekend but they seemed to be getting more friendly, and Letty couldn't risk being invited on the shopping trip.

By the time she was ready to go that evening she thought Nate had already left but as she walked to the end of the office a voice called, ''Night, Letty,' and she looked across to see Nate at Terry's desk tapping at his computer.

Wow, he did have his eye on everything. She wondered if Terry knew he did this.

She had a few bits to pick up for her overnight bag before she went home. Then there was a moment of panic as she got to her flat when she couldn't find her keys — she always kept them in the front compartment of her bag. Always.

It was a good thing her flatmate Ginny was in. Letty emptied her bag on the hall table, relieved to see the keys spill out of a different pocket.

'Phew,' she said. 'I must be more stressed than I thought if I put them in the wrong place this morning.'

'Stressed?' Ginny repeated. 'Sure, it's really stressful being whisked to London by a new man.'

'What's happening here?'

Letty had been hoping to cook something simple, pack, and chill in front of a film but Ginny had covered every surface with papers. Just what Letty didn't want to see more of.

'I'm putting all the household bills in sections and in date order.' Ginny waved at three new lever arch files. 'I needed to find an old bill and it took for ever. There's two years' worth lying about.'

'Good idea, Gin. I should do that too with my personal papers. My shorthand teacher has years of hers all sorted and lined up. It's impressive.'

Ginny passed her one of the files.

'You too can be impressive. I got you one for your letters from the bank and stuff.'

'Excellent. And can I smell something cooking as well? Is there a spoonful of that for me?'

'I didn't you'd buckle down without a bribe.'

'You know me well.'

It was satisfying, though, Letty had to admit. By the end of the evening one file stood bulging and the others had been started on.

'Look what organised people we are,' Ginny said, pleased. 'It'll be so good not to have to search for two days for an old bill.'

'Or struggle to remember when we had the electrician in last.'

Ginny looked around the now tidy room. 'Shall we put them on the shelf above the fruit bowl?'

'If we did one of those cupboards out,' Letty said, 'they'd fit in there. I don't think we want to be looking at them.'

'Absolutely.'

Letty yawned. 'Thanks for making me do this.'

'What's the man organised for the weekend?'

Letty hesitated.

'Hasn't he told you?' Ginny grinned. 'That's so romantic.'

'I don't know if we'll do anything special,' Letty said. She hoped she wouldn't have to make too much up when she got back. 'I'll be happy just to wander around.'

Ginny was still grinning. 'Of course you will.'

'What are you doing for the weekend?'

Ginny pushed the three files on to the shelf.

'I'll put these here, just for now. Tomorrow I'm going to start sorting that cupboard, and then I'm going home.' She laughed. 'Guess which one of us is going to have the best weekend.'

7

Letty felt apprehensive and not at all sure she was going to have a better weekend than her flatmate who would be doing ordinary, safe things. She felt nervous about being with Adam and worried he would be jumpy about what they were doing. And she knew they were both worried about Miss Kemp.

They checked in to the chain hotel Adam had booked, dropped their bags and met back down in reception. Letty had wondered whether there would be one or two rooms booked, but of course there was one each. Whether it meant Adam wasn't interested in her or he wanted their first time to be more romantic, she didn't want to think about. Maybe it was just good that he wasn't assuming anything.

'Someone recommended a vegan restaurant just down the road, are you OK with that?' Adam said. 'Then it's just one Tube line to the district where Fede lives.'

At least he was focused. Everything seemed bigger and noisier and much more crowded than in their small town and Letty was happy not to be asked to make decisions.

'London's so big! Everything seems like a longer walk than you'd think,' she commented later as he thought they were getting closer to Fede's address.

'I know.'

'And I don't know whether I'm pleased or disappointed that so many of the shops and cafés are the same as we've got,' Letty added.

'It's the same abroad, now, though, isn't it? There are British shops in Paris.'

'You're right,' Letty said. 'That's definitely disappointing.'

Adam pointed to a low, purpose-built block of flats. 'I think it's there.'

'Which one?' They stopped to look.

'I don't think we'll be able to tell unless we walk up and down and see the front doors.'

They found the number and stood for a long time looking, then Adam laughed.

'I thought I'd know what to do when we got here.'

'What do you reckon?' Letty said. 'We knock?'

She was afraid Adam would want to go away and maybe come back tomorrow. The only reason she would agree to that would be to make this easier for him.

He nodded and moved forward decisively.

'We knock.'

And knock they did — three or four times.

'I don't know if I'm starting to imagine things,' Letty said as they walked slowly away. 'But it felt as though there was someone in there.'

'You don't think we should ask the neighbours, do you?' Adam continued walking away, though, as if he'd decided they shouldn't.

Letty agreed. 'No,' she said. 'If she's hiding we should respect it.'

They came to a busy intersection and Adam walked quickly across with a lot of other people, leaving Letty on the central island. Some of the roads were very wide with the stream of cars and vans never ending. You could see why drivers wouldn't stop for you — they'd never get anywhere. The trick for pedestrians probably was to move quickly with the mass of the crowd as Adam had done. If, like Letty, you hesitated for a second, you were left standing. Clearly she wasn't much of a risk-taker after all.

Or she chose the risks that were worth taking.

She saw Adam stop and get his phone out and thought he was probably checking the map while he waited for her to catch up.

She felt the lightest of touches in the small of her back and froze. It was deliberate, not a normal jostling in a throng. Was it a gun? It was pressed very gently against her if it was.

'Letty, I am Fede Maldonado,' said a voice in her ear. 'Do not turn round. We may be watched.'

Letty didn't move. The touch on her back had disappeared but she could feel someone standing behind her.

'Rowena suggests meeting you tomorrow in the National Gallery,' the voice went on. 'Buy membership today so you can skip the queue and be there at ten in the morning. Room twenty-six, near the skittle players painting.'

She felt a draught behind her and looked over her shoulder as she crossed towards Adam. There was no one who could have been the person who spoke to her. No tall man walking away. No one who looked like a dancer. Where had he gone?

Had she imagined it?

No. She didn't know you could go straight into the National Gallery with a membership, and she couldn't have made it up that there was a picture of skittle players in room twenty-six.

If those two things turned out to be true, her mysterious contact would be right.

She had to explain it all to Adam twice before he could grasp it.

'That's brilliant, Letty. They were in there and Fede ran out. So they're afraid we're being followed — or that they are?'

'I'm not sure. Us as well, I suppose, if they want us to duck into the gallery quickly — but I can hardly believe it.'

'No. Anyway, let's get back to the Tube and find our way to the National Gallery.'

'You go for the memberships. I'll scout around and see if anyone is watching you,' Letty suggested when they had got through the security check in the gallery.

Letty wandered for a while, then stood beside Adam with her back to the counter while he finished the transaction. It was impossible to know. No one looked suspicious and she didn't recognise anyone from outside. Adam finished purchasing a year's membership for himself with the ability to take a guest in each time; that was a good solution. She hadn't thought, but you probably couldn't buy someone else's card for them and he wouldn't know her details. It was a pity though, because she'd envisaged herself later in the year saying, *We should go down to the National Gallery again, make the most of those memberships*. Instead he could take anyone: the woman he would have asked for help with Miss Kemp's personal items, perhaps. Or another friend, like Sam from work whom he seemed close to.

They located the place where they had to be at opening time in the morning — the painting was smaller than they anticipated — and then walked across Trafalgar Square.

'It's such a long time since I've been here,' Letty remarked. 'I'd forgotten that so many of the buildings are white and light-coloured. It makes it all feel very open.'

Adam looked at his map. 'I think that street is where all the ministries are but if we go down the next one we'll get to the Houses of Parliament and the river. Or was there something else you wanted to see?'

'No, let's do that.' A walk by the Thames was something she'd mentioned to Ginny, and to say she'd seen the Palace of Westminster would make it sound real. And a visit to the National Gallery would be worth talking about.

She didn't want to say anything, but Letty soon began to flag. They'd barely seen anything and she'd started to think sightseeing in London was too tiring to be worth it.

Perhaps it was the tension of what had happened earlier.

'Can we make our way to a bridge and see what else we can see?' she asked as they strolled beside the Thames. 'I'm not sure how much further I want to walk but it would be nice to see St Paul's — even if from a distance.'

'There's a bend in the river so we might not,' Adam said. 'Are you getting tired?'

'A bit. Maybe we could sit down soon.'

Adam looked at the time. 'I wanted to take you to one of the big shows,' he said.

That was unexpected. It would have

been a nice gesture.

'I think that takes a lot of forward planning.' Letty laughed, pleased he'd even said it. 'And you've already paid the earth for that gallery ticket. A London theatre would take the rest of your month's salary. I'm good without that, thank you.'

'The same person who recommended the restaurant got tickets for us at a small independent theatre — could you fancy a modern play, maybe a bit avant-garde?'

'I might not understand it but hey, yeah, theatre in London — what's not to want to go for?'

'She says it's not that type of avant-garde, just not a traditional theatre. It's about codes so I thought with your shorthand deciphering, it would have some resonance.'

'What, computer codes or more like Enigma?'

'Spies, I think. Shall we go for it?'

'Yes, let's.'

'OK — she's recommended another restaurant close to the theatre.'

'Good idea — we don't want to risk missing the beginning because of not getting across town quickly enough.' Letty was beginning to feel excited. And the good thing about London was, you were usually close to an Underground station.

Adam checked his map and they turned towards the Tube.

'Who is this friend? Does she live in London?' Or was she someone Adam went out with often? Or would take with him to get his aunt's toiletries?

'Yes. We were at uni together. I haven't seen her for years — but we're still friends online.'

'You didn't want to see her?'

'I didn't want to get involved in that sort of conversation, not knowing what we'd be doing, or have to answer questions about why we're here.' He took Letty's hand as they crossed a busy road and her heart almost stopped.

His hand was warm and dry. He wasn't indecisive at all. Except for the momentary faltering outside his aunt's friend's flat, she'd felt his calm steady certainty all day and been happy to follow him on this less known territory.

They sat side by side in the darkness of the auditorium and she could hear Adam laughing at the funny moments and leaning forward at a couple of tense sections. It was a young, energetic theatre company with a lot of movement and surprises and much humour. The set was basic but they conveyed the setting brilliantly with the little they used, the actors themselves dragging furniture round as if it were all part of the play.

Adam caught Letty's glance several times and took her hand again as they made their way with the crowd to the bar at the end.

It was impossible to talk in the tiny bar, crammed together with so many others from the audience, all, it seemed, speaking in loud voices.

'Did you enjoy it?' Adam asked as they left the little theatre.

They walked close together, but she longed for his arm around her shoulders.

'I did enjoy it,' she said. 'Though listening to some of the conversations in the bar just now, I think I may not have understood it all!'

'I know.' Adam laughed. 'Sometimes people like to read more into something than the writer ever intended.'

She smiled and nodded, and they carried on discussing the play — but was that what she was doing with this situation with Adam? Making more of it than there was? The way she had seen a sunset in a lot of coloured lines on first seeing the painting in Rowena's room?

They both hesitated in the corridor outside their adjoining rooms. It would be so easy for Letty to ask him into her room, but she overthought it for a second too long and he was moving away.

It was the right decision. He might be appalled at the idea — and there was still tomorrow to get through.

'Shall we meet for breakfast at eight?' she said. 'Eight-thirty?'

He nodded. 'Eight. Thank you for a nice day, Letty, if that doesn't sound too bad.' He gave a little laugh.

She laughed too. 'This is all unbelievable but thank you for making it — fun.'

She thought they both started to move towards one another at the same time, but he may have been a beat ahead. Their lips met in the briefest of touches and his fingers reached up to touch her cheek, then moved to the back of her head to play with her hair.

While her face was still upturned and his still close to hers Adam pressed his forehead to hers for a long couple of seconds, his hand still in her hair. Letty's breath caught in her throat and neither of them said anything.

Later, in her bed, Letty thought this contact had been the most meaningful of all.

* * *

They arrived as early as they could but Rowena Kemp was already sitting on the sofa facing the wall with the skittle players painting on it. With his back to her on the sofa that faced the way they came in was a man who could only be Fede — tall, slim, dark and very good-looking in an exotic way. There was a jacket, bag and books spread out beside him to deter other visitors from sitting down. Letty's stomach turned over. It felt like a spy film — or play. Very unreal.

Rowena looked as she always did, in casual trousers and shirt, her pixie haircut neatly styled. Letty thought she wouldn't want them to draw attention, so they skipped the hugs Letty knew both she and Adam wanted to exchange.

'How are you?' Adam asked, the words seeming too formal.

'I'm well, thank you, darling.'

He smiled. Letty thought he was pleased with the 'darling'.

'We found the documents you directed us towards,' he said softly. 'We can't find any trace of this —' he lowered his voice even more '— Ethan Marwick who is threatening you. Is it because you found out he was embezzling company funds or because he killed Derek Rawlings?'

Rowena nodded. So both things.

'And, Miss Kemp —' Letty began.

Her teacher smiled. 'Rowena.'

'Someone has broken into your flat and taken the rest of your files.'

Rowena gave a small smile as if she wasn't surprised. 'They got hold of a key somehow.

That's how they were able to take me by surprise.'

'They? Ethan?' Adam asked. 'Who else?'

'His wife may be working with him. And I believe there's a son, though he can only be about twenty.'

'Who hit you?'

'I didn't see but he said Ethan sent him. It may have been a hitman but then it could have been the son. He sounded youngish and wasn't very professional.'

Letty shivered. Someone more professional may have finished the job.

'So it wasn't true that you didn't remember anything?' Adam said.

'I'm sorry to mislead you, darling. All those years ago Derek Rawlings' family wanted a better investigation into his death and Ethan knew I had evidence of his financial irregularities and therefore his motive to kill Derek, but that was all we had. He threatened you, Adam, and me as well, so we got out of the country — especially we got you out. Then Ethan seemed to disappear from the radar.'

'You thought you were safe to come back?' Letty said.

'It was mainly because Derek Rawlings' granddaughter wants to reopen the case. She's a very clever young woman and thinks Ethan Marwick has changed his name but hasn't moved completely away. She asked me to come back and help and of course I was happy to. The man should be brought to justice — but we don't have enough quite yet.'

'You've brought him out of the woodwork anyway, Aunty. Do you think they meant to kill you or just frighten you away again?'

Letty looked at Adam. How extraordinary to be having this conversation.

Rowena's eyes flickered to the man sitting with his back to them. 'We've talked this over and it doesn't make sense to give me another warning if I've come back after the first one.'

'So why . . . ?' Letty couldn't say it.

Rowena could. 'Why didn't he finish me off? I think he was disturbed. There was a rather insistent banging on the door and Eva, my neighbour, called my name. He stood for ages listening near the door. I was so afraid he'd open the door and do something to Eva but I felt dazed and couldn't move.'

Adam took her hand. 'It's probably good you couldn't.'

She laughed. 'Yes, probably. I think he got out as quickly as he could.'

There was a pause.

'Fede said he thought someone was following — was it you or us?' Letty said. 'I'm guessing you think that's Marwick's people?'

'I'm not sure he actually has many people although I'm certain he has money and could move in circles where he could pay anyone to do anything and keep it anonymous. I've sometimes thought someone is watching me. Hopefully, Adam, they haven't worked out who you are yet. You haven't felt watched, have you? I'm scared they'll have realised now that you're helping me.'

'We'll be careful. I hope we haven't made things worse for you.'

'No, we need to break the impasse, I think. Derek's granddaughter is going to go public with the idea of reopening the enquiry and he'll show himself to make sure I don't testify.' She turned to Letty. 'I'm sorry I involved you, my dear. I thought the little note I left would be found by the police and transcribed as evidence. I was sure I was lying in a crime scene!'

Adam shook his head. 'They convinced themselves you had an accident and gave me the note.'

'How did you know to ask Letty?'

'It was a Thursday when the police called me and Letty turned up for her lesson just in time.' Adam beamed at her. 'I would never have unravelled what happened to you without her skills and insight.'

Miss Kemp beamed as well. Letty admired her so much for her ability to remain cheerful and calm in her circumstances. 'She's my star pupil.'

'Exactly how many pupils do you have, Aunt?'

His aunt brushed his arm away, still smiling. 'What's important for you two now is that you tell everyone I've gone back to Argentina and if the name Ethan Marwick is mentioned, you don't know it. Can you do that?'

'If they are following you they'll know that's not true,' Letty said.

'Very wise, Letty. Just in case, then, you'll need to be more vague and say I'm going overseas.'

'Do you know the names of the wife and son?' Letty asked.

'They'll have changed them. I've no idea about the son but the wife used to be Pamela. Actually, I'm not sure they were ever married so she had a different surname. I can't remember. It wasn't that dissimilar to his name. It doesn't matter.'

'It wasn't Marr, was it?' Letty asked.

'Do you know, I believe it was.' Miss Kemp looked shocked. 'Did you meet her?'

'No, I met her mother, who hadn't had contact with her for twenty years. It must either be because she died or she's become someone else.'

'Yes, I imagine Ethan Marwick could have family members looking for him too if that's what they did.' Miss Kemp laughed. 'Although maybe nobody liked him much. I never understood why Derek employed him. I always thought he was a nasty piece of work even before we found out what he was doing. But he was good at smiling and agreeing with Derek and he must have had something that attracted people, even if it didn't work with me.'

Rowena began to look around nervously.

Adam glanced around the gallery. 'Do

you think there's anyone here interested in us?' he asked.

'Maybe not but we don't want to risk making a mistake. If we're going to provoke Ethan into action, it needs to be on our own terms.'

Letty stared at Miss Kemp. So the risk was that Ethan would attack her in the wrong place, not that he might attack her at all. She wondered what playing safe would look like for Rowena.

'I'm sorry this is all so awful but I'm glad you've come back, and that you and I have found one another again,' Adam said.

Rowena reached out to him again. 'It's been a bonus, hasn't it?'

'How will we stay in touch?'

'I don't know. There's a part of me saying I'm making myself more important than I am and another part thinking they have the skills to intercept my messages.'

'Is he someone who would be good with technology, do you think?' Letty said. 'The son might, I suppose.'

'Ethan was, all those years ago. Whether he's kept up is another question. That's how he did the money transfers. I think he might have managed to pull any online information about Derek's death. Things may not have travelled so far so fast then but it's a lot of hacking.'

'Not all computer nerds are young.' Adam nodded to Letty. 'Your boss isn't, is he?'

'No, he and the deputy must both be in their forties, like Ethan.'

'So, how will we stay in touch?' Adam repeated.

'I'll contact you, darling, if you can be patient and try not to worry.' Rowena patted her nephew's arm.

'But if we find anything out?' Letty said.

Rowena hesitated for a long time.

'Let them have my pay-as-you-go number,' Fede said softly.

'But, Letty,' Rowena said. 'You are not to go looking for information. Promise me.'

Letty got her phone out to enter the

number.

'Just if anything comes up.'

Rowena stood up. 'Now, you go and see the Impressionists, or whatever takes your fancy.' She guided Adam round the seat and towards the exit to the room and said something seriously to him. Then she was gone, and Fede too.

Letty would have liked to say goodbye, but in a way she appreciated Rowena not making a big deal of the parting.

'I notice you didn't promise not to investigate,' Adam said as they made their way to the Van Goghs and the Turners.

Letty laughed. 'Did she make you promise?'

Adam looked sad. 'Not that. Something else.'

* * *

Letty slept on the train home. It was tiring going round art galleries but she'd seen some amazing artworks. She had seen reproductions of the *Sunflowers*, of course, but there was no substitute for experiencing the sight of one of the originals.

It was also tiring thinking their situation round in circles. When the train stopped at a station she opened her eyes briefly and found she was leaning against Adam's chest and he had his arm around her. From his even breathing she thought he might be sleeping too, but he tightened his hold on her when she stirred. She adjusted her position and settled back down so her head was on his shoulder. His skin smelled citrusy and of something else, masculine and indefinable.

They needed to talk about Pamela Marr, but here on a crowded train wasn't the place. She settled back again. This felt right. She decided on her five-year plan. A new job, definitely, and not in a purely money-making concern. And a steady relationship with Adam. They'd travel some more — Paris, definitely. Maybe they'd go to Latin America together, or have other adventures. There might be a day with orange blossom and champagne and then a cottage with roses round the door and swings and a slide in the garden — but it was best not to be over-specific. It felt perfect being beside him, and that was enough for now.

'This was bad timing for me,' Adam said as they parted outside the station. 'I have to go away again tomorrow.'

'For work?'

'Yes.'

'OK.' It was odd he hadn't mentioned it before and that he didn't explain more what it was about. Perhaps he liked to keep the different parts of his life compartmentalised. 'Let me know when you're back. We have things to talk about.'

'Don't forget what my aunt said. She doesn't want us to involve ourselves with her affairs.'

This was surprising. He'd said he had not promised not to, either. They couldn't stop now!

'How long will you be away?'

'A couple of days.' He turned to go.

'Let me know when you're back,' she repeated.

He raised an arm in reply as he walked away.

He'd be tired as well, and wouldn't be able to take it easier tomorrow. That would explain why he didn't want to talk more. Or kiss her goodbye . . .

It was still early when she got home and she was pleased Ginny wasn't back. She had a long bath and a snack, then sat doing some shorthand homework feeling very nostalgic. It had been nice to see Rowena, but things were never going to be the same again with her classes.

She glanced up at the clear shelf above the fruit bowl. Good. Ginny had found a better place for their files. This flat felt more and more homely. It was good to have this to come back to — whatever happened in other parts of her life.

8

'How's that shorthand teacher of yours getting on?' Maria wandered over to Letty's desk, unwinding her scarf.

Letty looked up, surprised. She didn't usually get so much as a greeting from a distance.

'All right, I think,' she answered. 'She's going back to — to where she lived before.' She may as well get some practice in telling the story. Perhaps Miss Kemp got her students via an agency and her employers would tell the agency. 'Abroad.'

'Is she? Do you know when?'

'She might have left already, for all I know.'

'Who told you?'

'I'm sure she will have let the company know,' Letty said, deliberately not answering the question. 'Or someone will have. Who from here arranges my classes and pays the fee?'

‘Claire does. She organised it all. Make sure she knows, will you?’

Maria went straight into Nate’s office and Letty got up and wandered down to see Claire. Claire and Terry had a space to themselves in the open-plan office, but slightly apart from the others. If Nate Wickham was at the top of a capital letter L, his deputy and office manager were in the side stroke at the bottom, close to the door and opposite the place where the workers made coffee. They both faced into the office, Terry’s desk in the corner and Claire’s slightly in front because of the filing cabinets in the other corner. Letty often wondered if it would be distracting always seeing people coming and going, and sometimes standing chatting while brewing up.

As she approached, Claire was standing by Terry’s desk and they were chatting and laughing. For a brief second, Letty wondered if she could wangle a role where she could share this space with them. It would be calmer and more fun than being stuck with Maria and having

Nate so close.

It depended on what she was going to decide to do now. It seemed absurd that her success in the company would hinge on continuing to learn shorthand, or that it ever had. She would tell Nate, or whoever decided these things, that she didn't want them to find another tutor for her.

She was beginning to think the whole idea of making sure she stayed here for a year, so it looked good on her CV, was pointless as well. If it was learn shorthand or go, she didn't mind going.

She wasn't interested in the work. Nate had treated her well and she felt a certain loyalty to him — and it would be hard to tell him she was leaving — but she didn't really owe him anything.

It was interesting how a weekend away made you see things differently, even when you hadn't been thinking about those things at all. Just a step outside of your normal life made things fall into place. She felt warm inside at the thought of the weekend, and of Adam.

Then in the split second when she saw

Claire grin at Terry and start to go back to her own desk, she knew she would start to look that very evening for something that wasn't all about making money and about secrecy. As friendly as Claire and Terry were with her, it wouldn't be enough to keep her here. If Adam wasn't able to contact her for a few days, at least a job search would occupy her so she wasn't brooding and waiting for him to call.

'Claire, Maria asked me to pop down and talk to you about my shorthand lessons. Is that right — you organised them and pay the invoices?'

'Maria made all the arrangements. Terry and I literally just pay the invoices as they come in.'

'So if they stopped, it wouldn't affect you?'

'You giving up then, Letty?' Terry called across.

'The teacher's leaving the country.'

'The one who just had that accident? Where's she going?'

'I'm not sure. She lived abroad before.

I wondered if she'd written to let you know, or if you need something in writing.'

'No. If she doesn't invoice she doesn't get paid,' Claire said. 'Just so long as Maria knows, as it was her contact and all.'

'Yeah — thanks.' Letty walked back to her desk. That was odd, both saying the other was responsible. But at least Miss Kemp wouldn't need to write a letter of resignation.

And at least Letty had made a decision in the course of working this out.

She went to buy a new notebook for her job search and then made her way to the café where Terry was sitting on his own at a table. She'd noticed Claire eating her own lunch at her desk as she left earlier.

'Claire too busy for a break?' she said as Terry waved her over.

'I'm a bit worried about Claire,' Terry said. He looked around. 'Well, and you as well, love. It's not a healthy company.'

'Isn't it? I suppose I don't have enough

to do with anyone else to realise.'

'You only need to have anything to do with those two.' He looked at her. 'The others can get on with their own clients but we don't have that luxury. Although recently I've observed rumblings among the others as well, not happy with how things are going. You're too kind, Letty, love. Both you and Claire should get out while you still can.'

'Why?'

'Because he's up to no good.'

'What sort of no good?'

'Yeah, Claire won't listen to me either.'

Terry gave a small laugh and Letty thought this odd moment would pass and they'd go on to talk about his family. But Terry moved his chair closer to hers.

'Not everything Nate Wickham does is, what can I say? — a hundred percent ethical.'

'Well, I think I realised that — but if the other companies aren't astute enough to see what's going on . . .'

'If the police got involved, it would be unpleasant.'

‘So do you mean illegal as well as unethical?’ Letty found her head was bent close to Terry’s and she’d lowered her own voice to a whisper. When he didn’t answer she added, ‘Why aren’t you getting out?’

He didn’t answer that question either. Letty felt her insides hollow as she understood. He was collating information to shop Nate Wickham.

‘See if you can persuade Claire to leave,’ was all he said.

‘You know she’s mainly staying to support you?’

Terry looked startled. Letty was certain she remembered Claire telling her she was staying because Terry needed the job and she felt she could help him. Evidently Terry hadn’t realised that. It was sweet they were both looking out for one another. His eyes flickered to the door and Letty followed his glance.

Of course — Maria would sometimes come in here as well. It was the closest lunch place to their office and the food was decent.

Letty sat back in her seat. Maria was looking at them but she didn't meet her colleagues' eyes.

Letty cleared her throat. 'How's the love affair with Midnight going?' she asked.

'Kate and I are now even further down in the pecking order,' Terry answered straight away. It seemed that his voice was louder than usual after the whispered conversation they'd had and suddenly Maria was in front of them.

'What are you two plotting?' she asked.

It was probably intended as a jest but Maria sounded deadly serious. Letty had often thought Maria didn't know how to joke.

'Terry's got a new dog,' Letty said, smiling, though she thought her smile might appear slightly stiff. 'It's replaced him in his daughter's affections.'

Maria nodded. She had no small talk either and clearly didn't know how to respond. She turned on her heel and left without buying a sandwich.

Terry and Letty sat on for a long

moment, each with their own thoughts.

'Better get back,' Terry said eventually and Letty thought he sounded as reluctant as she suddenly felt.

She was keen to get home that evening and get her laptop out to look for a new job. She thought honest, decent Terry was probably exaggerating the extent of her boss's wrongdoing and she'd be able to convince him to just leave as well. If he stirred things up, Nate might be angry enough to give him a bad reference and at Terry's age, he wasn't necessarily going to be top of the list for employment. Better to go on good terms.

Maybe she could look for something for him as well?

* * *

Ginny was home, opening cupboards, peering in, and closing them.

'Hi, Letty,' she said. 'What did you do with those files?'

'Me? Didn't you do that cupboard out and put them in there?'

'No, I couldn't be bothered on Saturday. I thought you'd got home early yesterday and done it but I can't work out what you've done with them.'

Letty's chest began to feel tight. She opened and closed every cupboard and drawer in the flat, mirroring Ginny's action. She even crouched down to look behind and under every piece of furniture.

Letty felt dizzy.

'Come on,' Ginny said. 'Where can they be? Either you've gone mad or I have. They were on that same shelf when I left for the weekend at lunch time on Saturday.'

Letty sat shakily on the sofa. 'They weren't there when I got back on Sunday afternoon.'

After a while Ginny put some music on and started cooking. Letty didn't want to frighten her flatmate with talk of what had happened at Miss Kemp's.

'Who else has copies of our keys, Gin?' She raised her voice to be heard over the music in the kitchen. 'The landlords?'

'Probably, but they're always super-sensitive about us being here when they send someone in.' Ginny stopped what she was doing and turned to look at Letty. 'And I don't think they'd have walked in over the weekend and stolen our bank statements.'

'Did we ever give them to a neighbour?'

'I didn't.' Ginny got on with chopping vegetables. 'Anyway, equally, why would any of them want our files?'

'You're right.'

'Oh, my sister's got a spare set, remember? Our safety net in case we were both locked out.'

'Where does she keep them?'

'Don't laugh but they've got a safe. Her husband brings stuff home from work and is paranoid about it getting lost.'

'Or shredded by the rabbits, I suppose.'

Ginny laughed. 'There is that. Or have something spilled on it.'

Letty forced a laugh, willing herself to

not let Ginny see her worry. 'Just wait, it won't be long till the twins learn the combination and can get the safe open.'

'Bless them, they're clever enough. But they aren't going to walk in and take our gas bills.'

Letty hesitated for a long time.

'Would you mind if I got the locks changed?'

Ginny seemed to be hesitating too and Letty got up to help with the food preparation. They always ate together when they were both home for the evening and Ginny was the more enthusiastic cook of the two. She would often batch cook and leave extra helpings in the freezer. She was such a good friend; the last thing Letty wanted was to make life difficult for her or frighten her.

'I'm really busy at work this week,' Ginny said. 'I don't think I can take any time off to wait in for a locksmith.'

'No, that's OK. I'll do all that, and get some spares cut, and tell the landlord. It's probably not necessary but I'd feel better.'

Ginny poked Letty in a friendly way with her elbow. 'Don't you want to leave it a couple of days in case they decide to walk back in with our files? We worked so hard.'

Ginny clearly wasn't worried and Letty thought she was imagining, despite having turned the whole flat upside down, that the files would turn up in an unexpected place they'd put them and not remembered.

'By the way,' Ginny said. 'There might be something else to worry about. One of the neighbours — Brian — grabbed me this morning and asked if our landlords were selling the flat. He'd seen someone who looked like an estate agent eyeing it up.'

'How does someone look like an estate agent?'

'Ha ha,' Ginny said. 'They all wear sharp suits and carry clipboards. Anyway, I got him to describe the person and she sounded nothing like that and got out of an ordinary estate car with no company name on.'

'Blue?'

Ginny stopped what she was doing.

'Do you know who this woman is?'

Blast. She shouldn't have asked the question that way.

'Not at all. I've seen a dark blue estate I didn't recognise parked outside. I think it's someone who goes to the new people over the road. What did Brian say the woman looked like?'

'Not very tall, short blonde hair. Is that who you've seen?'

'Yes, could be.'

'That's OK then,' Ginny said. 'Brian said he thought she had keys in her hand and she was coming in here.'

'Maybe she got confused and was on the wrong side of the road. The houses do all look pretty similar.'

'Yeah. Or Brian could have got it wrong, you know how vague he is sometimes.'

Letty hoped this conversation was over.

'Still, good to know he's looking out for us.'

'Yeah, it was nice. He didn't want us to go.'

Letty looked at the time again. It was too soon to ring Adam. He'd said he'd be away for a few days — but she should let him know. Why wouldn't whoever took Miss Kemp's files, and now probably hers and Ginny's, know who he was as well? Letty hoped it wasn't too late but wished they'd taken copies of some of the information from the other files. If they'd got into Adam's flat as well and the documents were lost for ever, Miss Kemp may not be able to testify against Ethan Marwick and he could get off for lack of evidence.

She went to her room to try his number and was diverted to voicemail. Letty sat with the phone in her lap for five minutes wondering what to do. Was it paranoid to think Adam's phone could be hacked and they'd hear his messages? After several more tries she left a voice message telling him she needed to talk as soon as he could manage. He was either very occupied with calls or had switched his phone off.

Maybe he'd been in meetings all day and had forgotten to switch it back on.

She sent an email as well just to be sure, but if he hadn't looked at his phone for texts he might not be looking at his emails either.

⋆ ⋆ ⋆

By the next day, once the locks had been changed and she was on her way out to get more keys cut, she'd revised her opinion of what could be happening.

He wouldn't be on calls all night and all the next morning.

He probably wouldn't switch his phone off for meetings, just on to silent, and if it was off he certainly wouldn't forget to turn it on again.

She choked back her hurt and disbelief. There was only one explanation. He'd blocked her.

That was what the talk of going away for work had been about. She'd thought it had come out of the blue at the time.

It was humiliating. Why couldn't he just have told her? After the way she'd been beside him trying to find out what could have happened to his aunt, she deserved better than just being cut out of his life with no explanation.

Whatever. She wasn't going to let Rowena Kemp down because her nephew was a coward. She would give Adam the benefit of the doubt for another twenty-four hours and then she'd get on with the investigation herself.

She had Pamela Marr's mother's phone number and the mother must have had some reason to believe Pamela worked near Letty's office. She'd talk to her and if she tracked the daughter down, she had Fede Maldonado's number as well. She'd tell him, and he could make what he liked of it that it was her and not Adam contacting him.

9

'Sorry it's taken so long,' Letty called to Claire as she walked past late in the morning. 'You did get my message earlier, didn't you?'

She'd called to leave her excuses on the answering machine before anyone would be in so as not to have to explain, and hadn't exactly rushed to work when the locks were changed. There was good reason for a diversion to Ginny's workplace to give her the new keys. Suppose Letty was delayed and Ginny was stuck outside?

Suppose Adam called and could see her that evening, and she had to say no because she needed to let her flatmate in?

'Yes,' Claire said. 'Household emergency. Not the electricians again, I hope.'

'Yeah, but it's fine now.' It was worrying when it became easier to lie, but what was the point of starting a discussion?

'Terry's had an emergency of some sort too.'

'Oh, do you know what's happened?'

'I expect he'll ring later if he can't get in.'

'Oh, you're here,' Maria said as Letty reached her desk. She held out a file. 'Nate wanted you to do this — the contract with the company you met the other day.'

'Ah, OK.' At least Maria had no interest in Letty's household emergency.

The contract had been drafted and redrafted and the latest copy was once again covered with the boss's scrawl. Letty smiled. It was almost easier to decipher her own shorthand.

Just a minute. This wasn't the draft she'd done — there were mistakes in it she would never have let go. Nate must have put some amendments in onscreen. Pity he couldn't have done them all.

It was good that he wanted her to be involved all the way through but he didn't have to make it this complicated.

She got out the notes on the meeting

and sighed. Nate must have spoken to someone in the company again without her knowing because some of the decisions had changed. Some of the figures were totally different.

Unless it was a test? It would be unlike Nate, she thought, but wondered if he was looking to give her more responsibility.

She'd been too distracted to start the job search last night. Could it be a sign that she wasn't meant to leave just yet? Unless he was trying to catch her out . . . but she didn't think he'd do that either.

She saved and printed two copies of the contract, one with the amendments and the second one annotated with what was different to the original understanding and calculations.

Later Nate came back out and passed her the contract back, not the annotated one, with two more changes. 'Thanks, Letty,' he said. 'You can delete the other copy of this.'

Not a test, then. Not a chance to be

given more responsibility. She was just supposed to trust that he knew more than her? Even if the figures he was now suggesting were so much higher than those that had been agreed?

Then he winked at her.

'Let's live dangerously, eh?'

She had to grin back at him. None of it was clear, but there was something about that roguish smile she couldn't help liking.

She checked for the thousandth time to see whether Adam had rung. He hadn't. She typed a quick text message, *Hope to speak soon*, and watched for a few minutes for the sign that it had been delivered to his phone.

That was it, then. If it wasn't delivered, he'd blocked her.

'No word from Terry?' she asked Claire on the way out.

'No, I'm popping to his house on the way home. Want to come?'

'If he's got problems he may not want both of us to descend on him.'

'Or he may want a bit of support,'

Claire said. 'I'll give him your best, shall I?'

'No, you're right. I'll come. It's on my way.'

By the time they were standing outside the front door Claire was looking worried.

'It's too quiet,' she murmured. Then, as the door opened, 'Terry, you look rough.'

He obviously hadn't shaved and there was a stain on the front of his shirt.

'Come in. We're a household in mourning.'

He led them through to a big, warm kitchen, where he was obviously in the process of clearing up after a meal it appeared no one had touched.

Letty glanced through to the other room where a pile of children of different shapes and sizes sat entwined on a sofa watching something noisy on the TV with little enthusiasm.

Letty didn't want to stare. Unless Rebecca was in the midst of them, she wasn't there. Letty started to feel anxious.

'What's happened, Terry?'

'So we always let Midnight into the back garden first thing. He went out this morning and must have got himself round to the front and got out. He's not home yet.'

'Oh, no.' Letty's hand went to her throat.

Claire sat down, then got up again and went in to the children. Letty got the impression Claire might be here often. She seemed to know the kids well. Letty could hear one of the younger ones crying. She started to pick up plates from the kitchen table and went over to the sink. She ran hot water and squirted washing up liquid into the bowl.

'Nobody's been to work or school today but it's been a disaster.' Terry was standing in the middle of the kitchen watching her. 'We've been out all together looking, and then in ones and twos all day, and have put posters up all round the district.'

'Do you think he got into the park, got confused and can't find his way home?'

Letty asked.

'I find that difficult to believe. He's not stupid. He wouldn't wander so far and if something frightened him, he'd bolt back into the house. I reckon someone's taken him but I can't say that to the kids. Rebecca keeps forgetting and looking for him. We'd just got tea on the table and she had a panic attack. Kate's taken her to the hospital.' He gave a smile that wasn't a smile and tilted his head towards the other room. 'I'm not dealing with this well.'

Letty looked for the used glasses and put them into the hot water.

'Do you want gloves?' Terry said, looking around helplessly.

'No, I'm all right. Has Rebecca had panic attacks before?'

'Yeah. It's frightening and she gets breathless but then she sleeps for a long time.'

'Sleep is probably the best thing when something like this happens. All you can do is hope for the best, and otherwise let time do the healing.'

'It's such a setback, Letty. She'd come on so well with the dog around. The others are devastated as much for Rebecca as anything.'

'You've got a nice family, Terry,' Letty said. 'He's not a noisy dog, is he? Could he have upset one of the neighbours with barking?'

'What, you think someone might have done something to him to shut him up? Nah. He barely barks at all and we don't often leave him home alone.' Terry scraped leftover food into the compost bin. 'Anyway, everyone commented how lovely he was with Rebecca.' He was silent for a moment. 'There's one I wouldn't put it past trying to poison the foxes, and then other animals could find it. But I don't know. They've got cats so probably not.' He stood thinking for a while. 'Anyway, this person was fretting about someone sitting outside in a blue car for hours — I don't think he'd have been bending my ear about that if he was planning to get rid of my dog.'

'Let's hope he just walks back in again.'

'Yeah. Thanks for doing this, Letty. I was frozen for a minute there and Kate would be furious if she came home to a war zone.' Terry brushed a tear away. 'Who am I kidding? It's always a mess here.'

'A happy mess, I imagine,' Letty said.

'And then I got a weird email from Nate Wickham. *Sorry to hear you can't get to work today. Hope the family are all right.* I don't know if it's a threat or not.'

Letty looked at him. 'A threat?'

So Terry was taking risks at work. She'd begun to think he wouldn't do that.

'Like, *you'd better be in tomorrow*.'

'Ah. Not a threat against your family.'

'Leave that pan to soak, love,' Terry said.

Letty pushed the issue a tiny bit further. 'He does seem quite controlling, the way he gets on to people's computers when they're not there.'

'Does he?' Terry seemed distracted.

'Yeah, he was even at yours the other day.' She gave a little laugh.

'What day?'

'Friday.'

Letty wondered what she was doing. Nate was always open about what he was doing. Terry wouldn't have found anything against him even if he looked. And Nate himself admitted living dangerously. If he was breaking the law, he wouldn't have said that to her.

Unless he was fonder of taking risks than she was.

Letty finished the washing up and wiped down the kitchen surfaces. She left them all watching TV and turned for home. Her plan was to arrange to see Pamela Marr's mother as soon as she could — tomorrow, if the woman agreed — and then concentrate on her job search.

The ideal thing would have been to talk things over with Adam — but short of that, what she most wanted to do was stop thinking.

* * *

Pamela's mother — Dawn, she said on the phone her name was — lived in a poor area on the outskirts of town. She was keen to see Letty.

Terry was back at work the next day but not saying much, and the atmosphere if anything was subdued. Or Letty imagined it so. She just wanted to keep her head down until it was time to go and see Dawn, and no one stopped her. Nate mainly kept to his office and Maria spent a lot of time tidying her desk.

As she introduced herself to Dawn and was invited in, Letty felt a bit of a fraud because she'd given Dawn to understand she could help her.

'After we left you the other day,' she said now, perched on Dawn's sofa, 'when we'd asked in all the other offices with no success, I felt bad. Tell me more about Pamela.'

'She's my only child,' Dawn began, her features softening. 'I thought we were close but when she was in her twenties she met a man.'

'Didn't you like him?'

'He was very charming but there was something false about him.'

Letty nodded. Maybe this was simply a girl cutting ties with her family to run off with a man.

'He was younger than her,' Dawn said. 'She hadn't had many boyfriends before and she fell under his spell.'

'So they ran away together?'

'Not straight away. They lived together in this very town and I would see Pam sometimes. Not him, though.'

'Did she seem happy?' Letty asked.

'Happy?' Dawn said the word as though she didn't know what it meant. 'Who knows?'

Not that close, then.

'Then one day she stopped answering the phone. I went round to their place and they'd gone. Nobody knew anything.'

'That's really distressing. When would that have been?'

'It was January of the new millennium. I felt as though she was starting a new life in a new year and new century and all of that. Or rather, he was, and taking her with him. I couldn't believe she'd do that to me.'

'Have you been looking ever since?'

'I got a private detective. The police wouldn't look into it — she was an adult, they said, and there wasn't any reason to think she was in danger from this man, however much I disliked him, they said, and I had to admit they were right. They made me feel like a person someone would want to run away from. But after a while I picked myself up and found the private detective.' She gave a little laugh. 'Imagine. Before that I thought they only existed in books.'

'Did he — she? — find any clues?'

'He. Some trails, yes, but they all went cold. What he did find out was that another investigator was looking for Ethan.' She stopped and looked at Letty with alarm. 'Are you all right? Can I get you a glass of water? Actually, tea, I should have offered you tea, you must have had a long journey. You don't live near here, do you?'

Dawn got up and hurried into the kitchen.

'No, that's OK,' Letty managed to say. 'Just a glass of water.'

'It's no trouble. I could do with tea as well, remembering all this.'

Letty got up to go with her. She'd be hopeless at poker, she reflected. It was clear to anyone what she was thinking.

'Ethan,' she said now. 'That's the name of the man Pamela was with, is it?'

'Yes.'

'So his family were worried about him as well?'

'There was something funny about it, my investigator said. The other guy let slip he wasn't working for Ethan's family. Someone else was trying to track him down.'

'They shared information, then?'

'For what it was worth. Milk and sugar?'

'No, thanks. So the other private detective didn't get any further than yours?'

'No. At least, not that I know.' Dawn lifted the mugs of tea and led the way back to the lounge.

'Why did you go to that building the other day?' Letty asked. 'Did you think Pamela was there?'

'Oh, yes, that's what I was going to tell you. The other detective has been on the case again — whoever was paying him has asked to reactivate the case.'

Letty sipped her tea, trying to control her excitement and hoping Dawn Marr couldn't hear the hammering of her heart.

'And he traced them?'

'He found something out, I don't know how. And shared it with my detective.' She laughed. 'I get the impression they both felt sorry for me.'

'Well, yes, it's an awful situation to be in.'

'So mine passed me that address on, just out of kindness. I thought it would be a house and I'd find them living there and they'd explain everything. Even when I realised it was offices, I thought I'd find her working there.'

'What work did she do?'

'She was a secretary. I was always a shorthand typist but I didn't want her to follow me into that. It's a dead-end job and doesn't even exist now, but she wanted to be like me.' Dawn laughed. 'Can you see why I couldn't believe she'd just up and leave me without a word?'

Letty cleared her throat.

'Yes, I can. Dawn, do you think it's possible they'll have changed their names?'

'Yes. That was the first thing the private investigator said to me all those years ago. But how would I know what they'd changed them to?'

'Of course.' Letty took a deep breath. She didn't want to spoil it now by appearing too eager. 'Have you got a photo? I can't go into all the other offices and stare at all the women who are the right age, but I may have seen her going in and out without realising.'

'I haven't any photos.'

'What, none at all?'

Dawn reached for a tissue. 'There was a break-in, years ago now. I shouldn't still be so upset about it. They didn't take much, but some of my personal stuff went. Stupid things like drawings Pamela had done at school that I kept, and all my photos.' She dabbed at her eyes, got up and went to pick up her handbag. 'This is the only one I have left.'

It was a small school photo of a little girl of six or seven. She had long brown hair tied in bunches but the photo was creased and faded, presumably from being handled so much. You couldn't make much of it at all.

'Could you describe Pamela as a grown-up?'

Letty took longhand notes to be totally sure she would not get any details wrong. *Five foot four, round face, long light brown hair*. You'd get your hair cut, wouldn't you, and dye it if you wanted to change your appearance?

Maria had never talked about a husband or partner and didn't wear a ring, but Letty felt she was close to finding Ethan Marwick. So close.

10

Letty's stomach began to churn again as she approached Adam's house. She was hoping against hope that he would react well to seeing her. At the same time she longed to see him, even if it was going to be painful.

At the very least Adam had to listen to her now — for his aunt's sake.

She slowed her steps because there was something happening up ahead. At first she convinced herself all the activity was to do with next door. Someone was having work done in their house and it had overrun, so the workmen with the white van were finishing it in the dark.

The blue lights weren't flashing on the police car so it wasn't an emergency.

But the police were there and kept her back nevertheless. She belatedly noticed the tape dividing the house off from the rest of the street.

'I'm a friend of someone who lives

here,' she said. 'What's happened?'

A young woman on the other side of the tape turned to her. 'Are you a friend of Adam's? Do you know where he is?'

'I only know that he had to go away for work but I'm a friend, yes. What's happened here?'

'We've both had break-ins. The front door and both the inside doors were broken so they're helping us make them safe.'

Letty could barely breathe. So they broke in rather than use keys this time. At least Adam hadn't been there.

'Was much taken, do you know?'

'Nothing of ours, as far as I can see. I'm waiting for my husband to get here and they're going to let us have a proper look.' She laughed. 'I couldn't really think straight to start with.'

'No, it must have been a shock. Can they not get hold of Adam?'

'I only had a mobile number for him. They're trying that. Oh, there's my husband now.'

A man was being allowed under the

tape on the other side and the woman ran across to him.

Letty stood helplessly for a long time and was about to give up when the woman came back.

'Adam's on his way, apparently. We're going in. They've made it safe and done their fingerprinting, they say. You can wait in ours if you like.'

'That's kind.'

'It's horrible being on your own when you come home to this,' the woman said. 'He'll need some support.'

Letty wasn't sure she was the one he'd want support from — the person he'd blocked from contacting him — or even that she could hit him with what she'd found out on top of this, but she thought she might burst if she didn't talk to him.

Her romantic side saw that it wasn't at all a good time if she wanted him to want to rekindle what they had, but that would have to take a back seat for now. What had they had, anyway?

The couple from the downstairs flat went to the main door when Adam arrived, a rucksack on his back. One police officer was left and they all went upstairs with him, Letty trailing at the back while the others explained what had happened.

The neighbours looked around Adam's tidy flat with interest.

'This is what ours is like,' the man said. 'Not touched. I always thought when they couldn't find anything worth stealing they made a mess.'

The policeman encouraged Adam to do an initial check to see whether anything was missing. He could let them have a list later when he'd had a chance to look properly. He left his rucksack in the main room and disappeared into the bedrooms, explaining about his flatmate being away. He thought nothing had gone.

Letty cast her eyes along the shelves. The two files of Miss Kemp's weren't there, but that didn't mean anything. He could have put them away somewhere.

Adam met Letty's eyes and gave a tiny shake of his head. She felt nervous as the others left. Was it going to be awkward?

At last they were alone. Adam turned to her and gave a little shrug.

'Of course it's the files that have gone,' he said. Letty searched his face for a sign of warmth but he was all business. 'We both knew they would be, didn't we? I can tell them tomorrow but I just need a moment to work out whether that's the best thing to do. I mean, whether it's too early to get the police involved.'

Letty nodded. 'You're right. There's such a lot of explaining to do and I wonder if there's anything they can do about it anyway. Especially now the papers we need are gone.'

'What do you mean, gone? Don't you remember? We took them out of the dated box files.' He picked up the rucksack. 'I've got them here. I took a copy and scanned them in at work and I've saved them in two different places.'

Her hurt at being blocked hadn't gone away, but this was important. He'd done well.

'You clever, clever person.'

He laughed. 'What are you doing here anyway?'

'I've got something to tell you too.'

Adam stood in the middle of the room as if wondering what to say.

'A glass of wine,' he said eventually.

'Um. OK.' Well, that was something. He wasn't sending her away.

After a moment he returned. 'Can't find any. Sorry. Would a beer do?'

'Sure.'

'I'm going to make myself a sandwich — would you like one too?'

'That would be nice.'

It would probably have been more sensible to refuse but Letty was hungry and her story may take a while to explain. Anyway, she thought Adam was using all this partly to put off the time when they would have to talk. She stood by the table, waiting, wondering if she could offer to help.

She watched as Adam found a frozen baguette, unwrapped it and put it in the oven. He set the timer then took the lids off two bottles. He carried the beers over to the table and put them down.

She waited until he was back on the other side of the room before she said, 'You blocked me on the phone, didn't you?'

He turned and looked at her. 'I promised my aunt I wouldn't involve you any more.'

'So that was what she asked you.' Letty sat down and took a mouthful of her beer. 'I'm surprised at Miss Kemp, thinking someone else can make my decisions for me.'

He looked thoughtful. 'You're right.' He turned back to what he was doing. 'You're right,' he repeated.

He seemed to take a long time making two filled baguettes and Letty stayed quiet. That was all it was? His promise to his aunt? She wanted to be relieved, but she'd been so badly hurt. How could it now mean nothing?

'And I'm surprised at you agreeing to it.' Letty startled herself at how angry she suddenly was. 'You knew how I felt and yet you caved in half a second.'

Adam turned to face her again, looking shocked.

'My aunt asked me,' he said. 'You know what she's been through. I couldn't argue with her.'

'Of course I know. That's the whole point. All of this has been to help her. How can it suddenly help her to shut me out?'

'It was what she wanted. She was thinking of you. She had your best interests at heart, Letty.'

'Maybe she didn't have all the information. You didn't question her decision . . .' Letty was struggling not to shout as all she'd been feeling tumbled out.

'It wasn't the time or place.' Adam looked white. Of course it was totally inappropriate to think he could have argued with Rowena in the National Gallery to keep Letty on the case, but that was what she wanted him to have done.

'You could have ignored her and explained later . . .' But Letty knew he couldn't have done this. 'You didn't even think to discuss it with me and you let me work out for myself that you were blocking me. How do you think that felt?'

She felt her voice crack on the last word and thought she was going to have to walk out.

She didn't want him to see her cry. But then they still needed to talk about Pamela Marr and Ethan Marwick. She wasn't going to let Miss Kemp down — though she felt a little let down by her teacher as well as her nephew. No one had any right to make her decisions for her!

Letty didn't move as Adam came to stand in front of her and carefully put his arms around her, drawing her close. She took a sharp breath in, surprised, but stood stiff beside him.

'I'm sorry, Letty. I shouldn't have blocked you,' he murmured against her hair, rubbing her back. 'I shouldn't have capitulated so easily when my aunt asked.' He stood back for a moment and looked at her, still not responding to him. 'I was worried as well that it all seemed to be getting dangerous and thought it was a good idea to keep you safe. I didn't think it through. I'm sorry.'

Was it enough?

'I should have known you'd disagree, should have let you make your own decisions. I did know.' He took his arms away. 'You were so important to me, I didn't want anything to happen to you but now I've messed up and I'm going to lose you anyway.' His voice was breaking, the way hers had earlier.

Letty felt short of breath. She couldn't see a way back from this.

Adam put his arms loosely around her again. Then he was kissing her urgently, as if he would never stop.

They were finished with words for the moment. Letty hugged him back and responded wholeheartedly.

As the kiss went on, Letty pressed herself against him. Adam sighed and drew away from her lips to plant small kisses on her cheek and neck. When the alarm rang to say the bread was ready, they both jumped. Letty would have happily let it burn.

There was silence while Adam finished the sandwich-making and carried the plates over to the table. Letty sipped her beer, watching him, hoping that what had just happened was the real truth of the matter.

When he sat down he held his hand to her back, near her shoulder, and she felt the warmth for a moment. 'I am so so sorry, Letty. I made a series of wrong decisions.'

She nodded, not wanting to rub it in.

'Please don't tell me kissing you was another one.' He gave a nervous laugh.

She reached across and kissed his cheek. 'That was one of your better decisions.'

He grinned. He'd been worried, then.

Miss Kemp had meant well, Letty understood that, and maybe the Letty she'd known could have done with protecting, but she saw herself stronger now and more determined. Adam had meant well, too.

'But don't underestimate me again or

treat me like a little snowflake who has to be protected.'

'Definitely not.' He turned back to his sandwich and lifted it to take a bite. 'I am sorry, Letty.'

'I know.'

'So, what's your news?' Adam asked after a few minutes.

'I might have found Ethan Marwick's partner.'

They were sitting on Adam's sofa and armchair by the time she finished, and Adam understood. He played devil's advocate for a while. She knew she would have done the same.

'But there's no indication this Maria you work with is married. You've sat in the same room as her for four months and she's never mentioned a partner?'

'She's an odd woman. We don't chat.'

'The mother didn't have photos. That's weird.'

'I thought that, but she said they all got stolen. It could easily be true. She was believable on every other front.'

'And the description doesn't really fit,'

Adam went on.

'Maria dyes her hair, I know it.'

'Shall we have coffee?'

Letty nodded and got up to get her notebook. 'I think we should contact the private detective.'

'Maybe. I'm guessing the other detective is employed by Derek Rawlings' family.'

'Me too. Your aunt did say they were re-starting the inquiry. So now they've got a lead, and we may have more.'

'I wonder how you get in touch with private detectives.'

'No idea. Do they advertise on Gumtree?'

'Gumshoe,' Adam said.

When she finished laughing Letty said, 'I'll just ask Dawn Marr for the details of her detective and see if he'll let us know who the other one is. Dawn said they both felt sorry for her.'

As she spoke, Letty was idly writing on a clean page in her notebook.

PAMELA MARR, she wrote and alongside that *MARIA PALMER*.

Adam came up behind her and watched as she crossed off the letters one by one, matching them letter by letter.

'Did the mother say whether Pamela had a middle name?' he asked.

'One that starts with I?' Letty said. There was only one letter in Maria Palmer that didn't appear in Pamela Marr. 'I didn't ask.'

Adam put a mug of coffee down beside her. 'What I don't understand is why they would have stayed around here. You'd go to a different part of the country. A different country. It seems like asking to be tracked down.'

'Unless you enjoy living dangerously.'

'This Maria doesn't seem the type.'

'No,' Letty agreed, writing and crossing letters out again. 'But I know someone who does.'

ETHAN MARWICK, she wrote.

And beside it *NATE WICKHAM*.

There was a buzzing in her head and she couldn't breathe as she started crossing out letters again. There was one left over. 'He's got a middle name that starts with R,' she said shakily. 'When I put a reference on his correspondence it's *NRW*.'

'Letty!' Adam was visibly shocked. 'You have to leave. You can't go back there.'

'They already know where I live. I didn't tell you this bit, but they went in and took some files from our shelf. It was only personal stuff and household admin but that was all that went.' She thought for a moment. 'They must have got hold of my keys. I thought I hadn't put them in the usual place one day, but it looks like they took them out and had more cut.' Letty felt sick.

'My aunt was right. You're not safe.' Adam was looking as if he felt sick as well.

'They took useless files — they'll see I don't know anything. It's you that's not safe, they took the actual files they wanted.'

'But the pages they wanted were missing. Will they interpret that as meaning I've got them or that I've not seen them?'

‘I’ll go to the gumshoe and you should lay low.’

‘I can easily have time off. You can’t. I’ll go.’

‘I’m going to spend the day in the office tomorrow complaining about a toothache.’ Letty laughed. She felt a little as though none of this was happening to her. ‘Let’s make it for Thursday and we’ll go together.’

* * *

As soon as she saw the detective, Letty realised the term gumshoe was giving her the wrong image in her head. This was no shabby little man. He was tall and well presented, smart in his plaid shirt and neat jeans. His short fair hair was fashionably styled.

He stood up and shook their hands.

‘Jonathan Walters. Jon.’

The other surprise was that he’d asked to meet in a café. There had been no climbing uneven stairs to a half-glazed door with his name on.

'Coffee?' Jon said, making for the counter. It looked as though he was known here.

Letty nodded.

'Soya milk, if they've got it,' Adam said.

'There's usually oat and coconut as well if you prefer.' He was on the ball as well as very courteous and friendly.

'Oat, please.'

He waited until the woman behind the counter brought their coffees over.

'So, what have you got for me?'

The investigator didn't have a loud voice but Letty glanced over her shoulder nervously.

'We can talk here,' Jon said. Letty had an image of him arriving early and interrogating the staff and other customers.

She dived straight in. 'You're looking for someone,' she said.

Jon nodded. 'Ethan Marwick.' He didn't lower his voice. 'My colleague said you'd found him.'

Dawn's detective had spoken to Jonathan Walters and made the arrangement to meet here. Of course he'd also told Jon what it was about.

'You're from the same firm?' Adam sounded as surprised as Letty felt.

'We've worked together on this case. You've found Ms Marr, I gather.'

'You've found Ethan Marwick, haven't you?' Letty said.

'Not quite, just hoping Pamela Marr will lead us to him.' Jon grinned and took a sip of his coffee. 'Look, my client is building a case to take to the police. I don't know what your aim is but that's all I'm going to do with anything I get from you — pass it to my client.' He paused. 'What is your aim?'

'My aunt was going to be part of the case against him,' Adam said. 'Rowena Kemp.'

'Was?'

'The last time they were compiling it. Still will, she hopes.'

'Pamela Marr was tracked going in and out of that building,' Jon said. 'That's all we know. She gives us the slip as she comes out but we think if we can track her home, we'll find Ethan Marwick.'

'I work in the same office as her,' Letty said.

Jon put his cup down and sat forward.

'She's calling herself Maria Palmer now.'

Jon raised his eyebrows. Letty thought he might be doing in his head what she'd done with the letters on paper.

'What office is this?'

'It's called Nate Wickham Accountancy Services.' She emphasised the Nate Wickham part and smiled at the expression on Jon's face. He may not be the greatest investigator in the world but his mind worked quickly.

They told him everything. He said he'd report back to his client and promised to ensure both Derek Rawlings' granddaughter and the police heard it all from them too when the time came.

'Oh yes,' Letty said. 'Do you or anyone else involved sometimes use a dark blue saloon car?'

'Why? Have you seen one around? It's not us.' He made a note in his book and then went on, 'This Rowena Kemp. Where is she now?'

'She's in hiding.'

'Good. You two probably need to step back now and make sure they think you know nothing.'

'I don't think they realise we've got the papers,' Adam said.

Jon looked doubtful as he fingered the USB stick Adam had given him. 'Be careful,' he said, standing up.

Letty checked the time on her phone as they followed him to the door and watched him walk briskly away.

'Oh, my mum's been ringing. Are you going back to work? I'll just see what she wants and walk with you.'

'Letty.' Her mother sounded agitated. 'I know you're at work. Can you get out to see your dad?'

'Sure. What's happened?'

'Something very peculiar. We were in the kitchen so we didn't see it but someone stopped their car outside and bent over and put something down over our wall. Rose from next door knocked straight away to tell us.'

'That is weird. What was it?'

'Rose thought it was someone's rubbish but she said they were quite careful how they put the bag down. The first thing we thought was that it was going to be a kitten. Do you remember, the same thing happened when you were little and we lived in that house with the hedge at the front?'

'Yes — Moses — he was a cute little thing to find in the hedge. So have you got another kitten?'

Adam gave her a questioning look and she grinned. Her side of the conversation must sound odd.

'No. It was three of those office files where you have to punch holes in your documents and slide them on to bits of metal.'

Letty stopped walking.

'Lever arch files. Three of them?'

Adam stopped with her and frowned.

'Yes — full of yours and Ginny's papers. Where could they have come from?'

Letty's head was buzzing and she said the first thing that came into it. 'Oh, it's a friend of Ginny's playing tricks on her, I expect.'

'What tricks? And how do they know where we live?'

'I know them from way back. It's a strange sense of humour.'

'It certainly is, and you can tell them from me it's not funny and we're not impressed. Anyway, your dad had to drive in to the dentist today so he's got them with him. Can you pick them up?'

'I'll arrange to meet him there.'

'He wanted to invite you to lunch but he's having an injection so won't be able to eat.'

'Thanks, Mum, we can all do it together another time. I'm so sorry this has worried you.'

'Go on, it's not a problem, darling. Warn your father we might have to talk about getting a cat now, though. I can't get little Mo out of my head.'

Letty laughed. 'Will do. Thanks, Mum.'

She ended the call and looked at Adam.

'Your files have been returned?' he said.

She nodded. 'Who are these people we're dealing with? One minute you're worried they want to kill you and the next they're giving you your stuff back.'

Adam didn't seem amused by this development.

'How do they know your parents' address?' he asked.

Letty thought about it. 'That is a point. They could have taken them back to the flat.'

'I guess this would be easier for someone than trying to sneak in the flat again without being seen. It doesn't feel like a warning to you, more them getting rid of the clutter.' He smiled. 'Not calling your files clutter,' he clarified.

'No.' He could be right that it didn't seem like a threat. 'Dad's down as my next of kin in the personal details I gave when I got the job.'

They walked on.

'I've got to go to the high street,' Letty said. 'It's useful that my dad's got an appointment at the dental surgery there, so I can be truthful when I say I've been to the dentist today. I'll need to buy a bag to put the files in, though. I don't want anyone to see what they are and have to explain why I'm carrying them.'

'It's five minutes' walk to the dental practice from my office and I've got a spare backpack there you can borrow.'

Adam turned off into a narrow street with low-rise purpose-built blocks on either side. If two people were moving in at the same time, the removal vans would have to back out as there would be no room to pass. And a private investigator couldn't park there to watch anyone's premises — they'd be moved on.

The office itself consisted of one large room, jam-packed with books, files and papers. It was rather as Letty had imagined the private detective's office might look, but the building was modern and everything was painted white.

There were four workstations,

although the two tables piled high with documents might have been desks as well. It would just take any worker who wanted to claim them a while to see the surface.

Letty grinned as she looked round.

'What?' Adam said, turning lights on. 'You think if anyone took anything from here, we wouldn't realise?'

She laughed. 'I didn't expect this.'

'I know where everything is.' He laughed as well. 'Or not. No, we've got new storage on order, it won't be like this for long.' He wandered over to a corner and poked at a pile of things. 'I think some of this is Sam's running gear.' He picked up a black rucksack. 'Will this do you?'

Letty nodded. 'Perfect.' She jumped as the door opened again and someone hurried in.

Letty had expected the co-worker to be a computer nerd from the same mould as the others she'd met — all young men, interested in computers above style and fashion. This was a woman, neat in jeans, jumper and a grey headscarf.

'Ah, here's Sam,' Adam said. 'Sam, this is Letty.'

'Hi, Letty.' The woman put a hand out. 'Samira.'

It wasn't often Letty felt big and clumsy. She was shorter than average, but Samira was tiny. Letty wondered what Adam had said about her — Sam seemed not to be taken aback by her presence here. She went over to one of the tidier desks, with a large screen and a desktop computer on it.

'The office furniture company rang and they'll be here this afternoon,' Sam said.

'I'll get out of the way then,' Letty said, moving to the door. 'Good to meet you, Samira.'

'Come back next week, you'll not recognise it.'

She wasn't at all what Letty expected, but she was sweet, Adam's co-worker. Did she need to worry about her? Was she the one Adam would take to get his aunt's things? They seemed very close, but she easily accepted Adam's girlfriend in her office.

Or maybe she didn't see Letty as competition.

Adam stood at the door with her.

'We should get together soon.'

'I wish we could have got the granddaughter's details,' Letty said. She'd been holding her breath but now needed to focus on the work they were doing. 'I'd love to talk to her.'

'Maybe we should let events take their course.'

Letty looked at him in astonishment.

'You don't mean that! I'm going to work on Saturday to make up for my time off. I bet Maria's address is on someone's computer.'

He didn't speak for a long time. Letty wondered if he was deciding whether to tell her not to. If so, he clearly decided there was no point.

'Let's go somewhere on Saturday night. To a club, or something normal people do.'

Letty smiled. They were a normal

girlfriend and boyfriend. Sam was a work colleague, no more.

'Great, let's,' she said. 'Somewhere with loud music so we don't have to think.'

'Good idea. I'll text you.'

'You better had this time.'

'Definitely.' Adam grinned. He pulled the door to behind him and drew her to him for a tender kiss. She forgot everything else and gave herself up to the depth of feeling in the embrace.

He held her for a moment after they pulled apart, as if he too was moved by the kiss. Her spirit soared at the thought of what might happen once Miss Kemp was out of danger and Ethan Marwick had been brought to justice. It felt as if they were so close to that happening now, she had permission to think of when it was all over.

This was nothing like any other relationship she'd had. Adam Taylor could be the one.

'Oh, and Letty?' he said softly. 'Be careful.'

11

As she stood in the middle of her living room and looked around, Letty knew she was fooling herself. She put the three files back on the shelf before Ginny got home that night, but it was too much to hope that she wouldn't notice. Sure enough, her flatmate stopped as soon as she entered the room.

'Where did they come from?'

Letty had mentally practised the story and it still didn't sound convincing.

'I'm really sorry, Gin. I was looking for somewhere else to put them at the same time as I was getting ready to go away on Saturday. I must have shoved them into the suitcase by mistake. I completely forgot.'

'You took them in a suitcase to London?'

'No. I was looking for something in it before I went.'

Letty could see a million more

questions chasing one another round Ginny's brain.

'What are you like?' was all she said, smiling, as she went into her bedroom.

Letty had lost count of the number of lies she'd told over the last couple of weeks. They were only to make sure people didn't get scared unnecessarily or stayed out of trouble, but they mounted up without you realising.

It didn't get any easier to tell them, though. There was another one on the Friday morning. She slipped into her boss's room first thing, trembling inside.

'I'm sorry I've had so much time off recently, Nate,' she said, worried about whether her voice made her sound nervous. 'I'll come in tomorrow to make up for it.'

'No need, Letty. You're a hard worker and everyone has health or domestic crises.'

'I want to make sure I finish those two reports and I won't have time today. It will be good to have some quiet time to get them done. Or do a lot of people come in on Saturdays?'

'I do sometimes,' he said. 'And Claire tells me she does occasionally. Not usually anyone else.'

Darn. She could only hope neither of them chose to turn up tomorrow.

* * *

She thought more about the consequences of lying and pretending on Saturday morning. The problem was, it didn't fit with her way of being. She was certain she looked guilty just going in to work. The only reason Ginny hadn't called her out the other day was because there was no space in Ginny's world for her to even imagine Letty would have invented the whole story around the files. Letty remembered that she was like that once.

The office was dim and quiet, apart from the hum of machinery.

The two reports weren't going to take more than an hour each, once she got going. She powered up her monitor and then jiggled the cables so that it went off.

She walked down to the coffee-making area and put the kettle on, then, as if she'd just thought of something, went across and switched Claire's monitor on.

Act normal, Letty, she told herself. She knew no one could be watching her. They couldn't be, could they?

Coffee mug in hand, she settled herself on Claire's chair. Sure enough Claire had taken the photo in the frame away, ready to put a newer one in. Her desk looked empty without it. Letty began checking Claire's files, remembering the conversation they'd had about passwords.

'I can never think of good ones,' Claire had told her. 'Nate complains mine are too obvious.'

'Nate knows your passwords?'

'He's the IT coordinator, he knows everyone's passwords. You might not have been here long enough yet but every few months he'll come round and nag you to change it to maintain security and he won't like it if it's what he calls weak. Anyway, he needs to get into the personnel files I've got.'

'And, what, you use your nieces' names and birthdays?'

'No, I'm not that daft. But things like animals I like. How Nate ever found out I like koala bears I'll never know.'

Letty had laughed. 'Everyone likes koalas.'

'So what do you use?' Claire had asked.

Letty could only hope today that Claire had used the idea she'd given her last time. She thought her heart would beat its way out of her chest as she keyed it in. *Not recognised*.

She stood up for a moment and looked over to the door, mentally measuring how many steps it would take to get there. She'd hear if someone swiped in, but didn't know how quickly she could close a file down if Nate walked in and swiftly over to stand beside her. She moved Claire's monitor so no one else would be able to see it, at least not straight away. It struck her that Terry would be able to see what was on Claire's screen at any time without really trying.

She wondered if Claire knew what Terry was doing. Possibly not, because Terry seemed so open and honest you wouldn't expect him to be keeping secrets. Presumably Claire really wasn't keeping secrets, with her screen so freely available for him to see. Anyway, hadn't she said Nate got into her files whenever he wanted to?

She hoped Nate wouldn't check next week and find files had been opened on Saturday. Her insides felt leaden.

All the more reason to get this done quickly. Then it really would be all over. And there was tonight to look forward to.

Sitting back down, Letty recalled the way she had recommended Claire change one of the letters in her password to a capital or substitute a figure. She stopped breathing as she made two more attempts.

Amazing. She was in. She didn't know how many tries you were allowed. Claire was fairly predictable and played safe.

She must remember to ask again about the new look Claire was planning — she hadn't seemed keen to talk about it before, but she'd been so enthusiastic when she was talking about her trip that Letty felt she should remember to ask again.

What they hadn't talked about was naming files and within her folders, Claire's were strings of numbers.

It didn't matter. Literally the only thing she needed was Maria's address — and if possible, Nate's as well.

She tried all the files containing pay details in order. It would have been interesting to see how much the consultants earned but that would just waste time. Here it was, somewhere near the middle of the list of files. *Maria Palmer*. Letty scribbled the address on a scrap of paper, folded it and jammed it into her jeans pocket. It was an out-of-town address. Maria had a long journey in.

Now she started from the end, hoping they were listed alphabetically. Yes, here it was. Nathan Robert Wickham — so

Claire did his pay as well. It would be fascinating to know how much he paid himself, but she just needed the address. Hah. The same as Maria's. So Claire had known all this time they lived together! She was very trustworthy, never breathing a word.

Letty took a huge breath and let it out — and before she'd exhaled completely, there was a sound outside and someone was coming through the door.

She closed the file and folder down.

Nate looked more casual than usual, in faded blue jeans and a light blue shirt. He was carrying a large holdall as if he was on his way to the gym. There was no doubt about it, he was an attractive man — and if he worked out, that would explain why he looked so youthful. She wondered how he managed around women if he never let on he was in a relationship.

She wondered what he saw in Maria.

'Oh, 'morning, Nate.'

'Letty. Why are you sitting there? Is Claire here as well?'

'No, I couldn't get my monitor to start so I was wondering if I could get into my files from hers. I've only just arrived myself so I haven't had a chance to test it out yet.'

'You should be able to, so long as you can remember your password. But what's wrong with yours?'

'It wouldn't start.'

He walked up the office. 'Why use Claire's?'

'I thought some of the others might object if I touched theirs. I don't know them as well as Claire.' She hesitated. 'And I knew Maria wouldn't like it if I sat at her desk.'

'Yes, you won't want to upset Maria next week.' He switched Letty's monitor on and walked around, checking connections. 'There you go. One of the cables had come loose.'

'Oh, brilliant.' She watched it spring into life. 'Actually now I come to think of it, that happened once before, in my first week. The cleaner had knocked it out or something.'

'Hmm. I'll just be in my room for an hour.'

'Want me to make you a cup of coffee?'

He looked back at her, one hand on the door to his office. 'No, you're all right — thanks, Letty.'

Letty got on with her reports and made slow work of it because she was trembling inside and out. Suppose he had a gun in his drawer as Rowena did? He could come out and shoot her. Only Adam knew she was here. Well, he knew she'd said she would be coming, but no more.

For the first time, Letty seriously regretted moving her desk round. Every time there was the slightest sound of the building settling down around her, she could feel her back tingle with the expectation of a shot being fired.

* * *

After an hour or so Nate emerged.

'I'm off now, Letty. You should leave

too. It's not nice to be here on your own. You can finish that on Monday.'

He put the holdall down — it seemed heavy — and stood and waited while she got her things together. It was impossible to argue with him.

So he didn't trust her.

Or he was looking out for her welfare.

'Thank you, Nate. I appreciate your concern.'

'No worries.'

He accompanied her out of the building and she could feel him watching as she walked away. She made her way into town and spent a few hours trying to calm down by looking around shops and mingling with the crowds.

By six o'clock Letty was home and having a feeling of déjà vu. Adam hadn't got in touch with her that first weekend because she'd made him think his aunt might have been attacked, and he couldn't face it. Better to keep imagining she was ill or had an accident. It wouldn't be that this time — he was right beside her with their knowledge that

Ethan Marwick was involved in seeking to harm Rowena to continue covering up his probable murder of Derek Rawlings.

Not only that, Adam liked her. Really liked her if she wasn't mistaken. This was the start of something important, special . . . she knew it.

Letty shuddered at the thought of being alone with Ethan Marwick that morning. She felt sure he couldn't know she was involved in anything Rowena Kemp was planning related to his past life, but she was shocked that she'd still been able to think him helpful and considerate. The ability of the man to charm her was amazing. It was as though he put a spell on her.

At least Adam hadn't blocked her this time, but he wasn't answering his phone and hadn't answered her texts since Friday lunchtime — just a jokey comment about the club they'd fixed on to go to tonight, and an observation on something in the news.

If he'd lost his phone he'd come in person to see her, surely, or find a way to send an email. She tried to think whether he actually knew her address.

She was feeling decidedly unsettled. She could go to him. It was only fifteen minutes if she went across the park, and it was still light.

She laughed to herself as she imagined his phone under a pile of papers in his office, buried too deep to hear it ringing.

'You look pleased with yourself,' a voice called and she looked up to see Terry balancing five supermarket bags as he made for home.

She smiled. 'Not particularly, just a funny thought.' She relieved him of two of the bags and began to walk beside him. 'How are you all?'

'Oh, you know.'

'Yeah.'

'This is the shopping we should have got this morning and the day's gone by and the cupboards were still bare. Good job supermarkets stay open so late now.' He looked at her sympathetic expression. 'No, no, it's not that we're too depressed to get going. We might be overcompensating with other activities, though. We're still walking the streets as well and knocking on doors.'

'No news?'

'Nothing. Come in and have tea and distract Kate for half an hour. She'd love to meet you. Or a glass of wine, I've no idea where the yardarm is any more, let alone whether the sun's over it or not.'

Letty felt sorry for this family. She could spare half an hour.

What she didn't expect was half an hour of fun and laughter, including funny stories about what Midnight did, even Rebecca sitting smiling at the table crumbling a piece of cake, before being whisked off by the younger children for a boisterous game.

'You look a bit shell-shocked, Letty,' Kate said, getting up to go and check they were all all right. 'Our lot when they're on good form are sometimes a bit hard to cope with.'

'It's good to see how resilient they all are,' Letty said.

Kate looked pleased. 'Yes, they are,

aren't they? Now, have another cup of tea and you and Terry can have a quiet chat.'

'Did you think any more about leaving work, love?' Terry asked.

'I am thinking about it. How about you?'

'Me too. I think the end may come sooner than I expected.'

'What end?' Letty felt a pang of fear for Terry. Did he think he'd been found out?

'Keep it under your hat but I think Nate's planning to pull the plug.'

'How?'

'Seriously, Letty, don't tell Claire. I don't know how far in she is with him but Nate's been putting money in an account abroad and might be planning to move there. Big money.'

Claire was 'in' with Nate? Surely he couldn't be right about that.

'He's going to abandon the company?'

'Precisely. And there's no one to keep it going, even if he was leaving the funds for it. You might argue he's the boss so it's all his anyway but it feels as though he's stealing from the company as well. So we'll all be out within a month of him going. I don't think I could keep it functioning on my own, not as the consultants would expect.'

'But he's not keeping it quiet if you know.'

'I dug quite deep to find out.'

'So he doesn't know you know?' As soon as she said the words, Letty thought of the missing Midnight and realised she was wrong. She stared at Terry. 'Midnight. It's Nate warning you off.'

'And I told him I got the message. We had an uncomfortable talk about the dog going missing but we both knew that wasn't what we were talking about.'

'You're sure he understood you're not going to pursue it? You're not, are you?'

Terry shook his head.

'He knows I won't take chances with my family. It's a cop-out but if he's doing a moonlight flit soon anyway I figure it's only money, so let him go.'

'Why do you think he's going now?'

Letty asked.

'I've always thought he had a past that was going to catch up with him.'

So Ethan Marwick was going to reinvent himself again. 'Do you know anything about that past?'

'No.' Terry laughed. 'Only in my imagination.'

'Is it the Cayman Islands?' she asked.

'What? No. Oh, you think the money's going to a tax haven. No — Malta.'

Letty stood up. 'I'd better get on with my job search then.' She stopped. 'What makes you think Claire is working with him? She seems nothing but supportive of you.'

'Yes, so you said. I think that's a way of checking what I'm doing, finding out how much I know.'

Letty headed slowly for the door. So despite the positioning of their desks, it was Claire checking up on Terry rather than the other way round.

'That's shocking, Terry.'

Was that what the visits to this house were about as well? Letty hoped there was some honest friendship as well.

'If he found out,' Terry went on, 'it wasn't because I talked about it to Claire so he's obviously got other ways. We're all hiding something.'

Letty was conscious of how much she was hiding and wondered if Terry recognised that. She wanted to tell him she would explain her secret as soon as she could, but there wasn't any point in involving him at this juncture.

Anyway, just admitting she had a secret, if it were whispered in the wrong ear, could be a mistake. Besides, Terry had enough of his own problems.

'Kate, thanks for tea and cake,' she called into the house and then to Terry, 'Good to see them all again.'

Of course it would be harder for Terry to get over the loss of Midnight. He knew he was the one who was responsible, and she could bet he hadn't discussed with Kate what he was doing. There was a leaden feeling inside her as Letty remembered she'd been the one to tell Maria about Midnight. She was responsible in this, too.

Letty checked her phone as she left the park. Still no word from Adam, and there was no answer when she rang the doorbell. Nor any feeling that there was someone inside.

The downstairs neighbours were in, though, and remembered her from earlier in the week. They invited her in.

'I don't want to disturb you, I just wondered if you'd seen Adam or knew where he was.'

'No, we thought he might have gone away for the weekend again,' the woman said.

'Did you see him going out with a bag?'

'Well, no, we don't watch his comings and goings but in these flats you sense whether there's anyone upstairs or downstairs and I don't think he's been there at all today.'

'When did you last see him?'

The couple thought about it and the woman answered first.

'Friday morning he went out at

eight-thirtyish. To work I imagine, as normal.'

'Yes — I met him at the door,' the man added. 'I sometimes do at that time.'

'He might have got home late,' the woman went on. 'He's very considerate and will be extra quiet if we're in bed, and he could have gone out again early this morning, but I reckon he hasn't been here since Friday morning. Are you worried something's wrong?'

'No, not particularly. I was afraid he'd lost his phone and couldn't get in touch — we were going out tonight. But he could have been called away, I suppose. I'll post my number and address through his door just in case but there's sure to be an explanation.'

'Sure to be.' The woman went to the door with Letty. 'So, how long have you known Adam?'

'Oh, about, um, about a month, I suppose.'

She knew what this woman must be thinking now. She probably wouldn't agree to take Letty's number and get in touch if she saw Adam.

The woman nodded. 'OK. I hope it works out for you.' She closed the door gently.

12

She'd known Adam for less than a month, Letty reflected as she took the long way home. Three and a half weeks. Was that a reason not to worry about his welfare?

She'd rushed round to check up on him before, only to find that he'd been fine but had made the decision not to involve her any more in helping his aunt. Yet he'd understood that had been a wrong decision — hadn't he?

Suppose he'd been rethinking the matter and decided again that they shouldn't be in touch? Not blocked her . . . but he could be ignoring her.

Every fibre of Letty's being cried out at the idea.

They'd talked it over — had their first row, even, and made up. Anyway, Adam wasn't a philanderer who would kiss her the way he had on Thursday, text chat and jokes on Friday, and decide to ignore her on Saturday.

But his downstairs neighbour was right to be cynical. A month was nothing — and a lot of that month had been spent investigating something else, not sharing life stories. Still, it had been an intense time and you get to know the essence of a person through those experiences — don't you?

Practically, though, she knew nothing about Adam Taylor except that she was falling in love with him. Not enough to ring around hospitals to see if he was lying injured there. Not his medical history or date of birth, not whether he had any identifying marks.

No — risky or not, she had to contact his aunt.

It took an hour to get the message right.

A missing 24hrs L

Now there was nothing she could do till Fede or Rowena replied.

She plugged her phone in to make sure it was charged and she wouldn't miss a message or call when it came.

* * *

What did arrive the next morning, as Letty was trying to eat breakfast, was an email from an address she didn't recognise. She felt the taste of fear for a moment until it became clear who it was — Sam and a string of numbers could only be one person.

Hi Letty, the message read.

Sorry to write out of the blue, tell me if it's inappropriate. I'm Sam, who works with Adam. We met in the company offices last week.

I'm worried about Adam as he hasn't been in touch since Friday. The furniture we'd ordered, that we were expecting when you were here, kept being delayed. I had to leave, Adam stayed to take delivery and I haven't heard from him since. Or received answers to my texts and emails.

I've come into the office today and the furniture is here all right. I don't mean to worry you, Letty, but I've managed to get into his email and thought I'd see whether you have any idea where he could be. It's so unlike Adam not to respond.

Thanks. Sam

It was marked as sent only ten minutes before. Letty wrote back straight away.

Sam, I'm worried too. Are you still in the office? Can I come round to talk?

Yes, Sam wrote back. Will be here for a while.

* * *

The new shelves and filing cabinets were obviously second-hand. Of course a company like Adam's wouldn't be able to afford the pristine new furniture Nate Wickham could. Letty felt a twinge of nostalgia for her old workplace with its mismatched desks and supportive atmosphere.

'What happened?' Letty asked.

'OK — you were here Thursday and the filing cabinets were due to arrive that afternoon, but they rang to say it wouldn't be till the next day.'

'The shop itself was going to deliver?'

'Yes, that second-hand office furniture

shop on the corner of Ruby Road, do you know it?'

Letty shook her head.

'I don't know if they deliver or employ someone to do it. We've used them before and they're usually great. But on Friday it started to get late and I had to go so I left Adam here. We arranged that he'd message me when they were here and he would spend most of Saturday sorting out here. I know you guys were going out in the evening.'

Letty nodded, smiling. He'd already been making sure his schedule for the next day was cleared. 'And under normal circumstances he would have messaged?'

'Always, even if they didn't come. He wouldn't have kept me in the dark.'

'But they did come.' Letty surveyed the office.

'I even rang the shop to see if they'd confirm who did the delivery but they're obviously closed at the weekend.' Sam's pretty face was concerned. 'I don't know what difference it would make. The furniture came and Adam took it in. It's what happened to him after that . . .'

Letty felt an immediate affinity with Adam's colleague.

'I do that,' she said. 'Ask questions and work out if it means anything later.'

'I'm concerned this could be to do with his aunt who got hit in her flat. Adam tells me it's a very long and old story, but I know someone was threatening the family years ago and he was hoping all that hadn't reactivated. He was just pleased his aunt was safe and he wouldn't engage in any discussion about whether they could be coming for him. I thought he genuinely believed they weren't — and Adam's not someone who can lie or easily hide what he thinks.'

That was true, Letty had to admit. Not like the way she was becoming! But now wasn't the time to worry about that.

'He might have convinced himself he'd be all right,' she suggested.

Sam laughed. 'The power of autosuggestion.'

'Are these other units all offices, or are some of them residential?' Letty asked.

'These were all built with a flat attached to the office space. Some of the business owners live over the shop,' Sam said. 'There's a tiny space in the back here that one or other of the directors who live out of town use sometimes for an overnight.'

'Directors?'

'Well, we're all directors. Does that sound pretentious? What does Adam call them?'

'Part-time workers. Maybe that was just a way of explaining the set-up to me. I get it that you all have a joint stake in the business.'

'Anyway, our residential bit is tiny and we all use the kitchen and bathroom, but I've seen one of the upstairs units and two people could easily live there and have a private life apart from the office. Then they only have five steps to go to work in the morning.'

Letty hesitated. 'You've checked the flat here, haven't you?'

'To see if Adam was lying there unconscious?' Sam gave a hollow little laugh.

'First thing I did.'

Letty nodded. Good. Sam was thinking along the right lines.

'I think we should maybe ask the neighbours if anyone was here and if they saw anything.'

Sam stood up. 'I like your style.'

* * *

In Adam's block, a few people had seen a white van outside around six o'clock on the Friday. They remembered the time because they'd all reflected how deliveries came at all hours these days. At the lower levels of the block opposite, they confirmed the time. Someone even saw filing cabinets being carried in. Two delivery men and a driver with a sheet of paper. Nothing to distinguish them. No markings on the van that they could see.

Letty was pleased Sam didn't flag as they continued going systematically from one door to the next, or say there was no point carrying on. At one of the units on the top floor, they thought there was going to be no answer and they had all the information they were going to get when a voice from inside called, 'Just a minute.' Eventually the door opened to show a tall young man with his foot in an orthopaedic boot. He had a short beard and thick, dark hair.

He saw them look him up and down and smiled.

'Don't ask. A sad story of home gym equipment getting its revenge.'

'Ouch,' Letty said, smiling. She saw that Sam was amused too. You couldn't help smiling at this laughing face despite the sad story and despite their own concerns. 'We're just asking around to see whether anyone saw anything unusual in the street on Friday around six o'clock.'

'Are you police?' He looked at them doubtfully.

Letty could imagine that the pair of them looked nothing like police.

'No. Our friend's gone missing.'

The man nodded, looking serious now. 'Would you mind coming in?' He held the door open. 'I can't stand for very long.'

Letty exchanged a glance with Sam, who was looking excited. Might they be getting somewhere?

The room they walked into was a similar size to the office in Adam and Sam's unit, but held only one very large desk and was an oasis of calm and order in comparison.

Behind the desk, an easy chair had been placed by the window with a soft footstool in front of it.

'As you see,' the young man said, 'I've got a place to watch whatever goes on in the street here.'

Letty laughed. 'And I'm hoping you were settled there on Friday.'

'Could you turn that chair round?' — he gestured to the office chair by the desk — 'and haul another one over and we'll settle ourselves here now. Shall we introduce ourselves? I'm Jamal. You'll understand why I can't offer you any coffee.'

Letty had only had half a cup at breakfast and that seemed like a long time ago.

'I'm Letty and this is Samira,' she said, pulling a chair over. 'If you want to take advantage of our presence to make you some coffee, just say.'

Jamal's face lit up. 'Would you?'

'I'll do it,' Sam said. 'I work in one of the lower units over the road and I'm dying to see what your kitchen's like.'

'State of the art, you'll see.' Jamal laughed. 'Instant coffee only, but it's fair trade.'

'So,' Jamal said, when the coffee was made. 'I've told all this to the police.'

'Did they come round talking to everyone?' Letty asked.

'No — I called them.'

Sam glanced at Letty and she thought it meant *Stop with the questions until he's told his story*. She nodded.

'So I'm sitting here and a white van draws up. A man with a piece of paper gets out and goes into the building opposite. He comes back out, opens the back of the van and two other men start carrying filing cabinets out. It wasn't a massive vehicle but was one of those vans where you can pull a ramp down, and they had trolleys.'

'Yes,' Letty said, though Jamal clearly didn't need any encouragement.

'There's a woman downstairs from me who sometimes brings her two boys to work,' he went on. 'They're nice little kids but curious as anything. I think she must have locked her unit then remembered something and gone back for it. Well, the kids were waiting in the street and the older one went over to the back of the van.'

Jamal took a sip of his coffee, evidently enjoying having all their attention. 'Then a lot of things happened at the same time. The two who'd been doing the heavy lifting came out, there was a bit of chat with the driver and they went round the front of the van and got in. Another man had come out with them and there's a bit of chat with him and the driver gets him to sign a piece of paper. I noticed, because usually you do an electronic signature now.'

Sam laughed. 'Yes, usually in a really

tiny amount of space.'

'Yes.' He smiled at her. 'So while all this is going on, the littlest kid is running up and down the ramp. The driver wouldn't have seen because they're standing at the front of the van. I took my eyes off of the child and then the guy who's signed follows the driver round to the back of the van. I think the driver called him over. The driver flips the ramp up, punches the guy who's signed in the face, and as he falls against the back of the van the driver gets hold of his legs and manoeuvres him up and shoves him right in. Then he slams the back doors shut, races round to the front and hares off.'

'What?' exclaimed Letty.

'That's what I thought. It took me a minute to process what had happened, then I'm on my feet opening the window and trying to wave my crutch out of it to get someone's attention and counting little heads on the pavement. And cursing myself for my broken foot because I could have been down there.

'Then the woman comes out of her unit and starts screaming and rushing around and I'm calling 999 and yelling at her to come up.'

'How many heads?' Sam asked tensely.

'Just the older brother.'

'The little boy was in the van?' Letty asked.

Jamal shrugged. 'Wasn't in the street. I had to limp down in the end, but the police — to their credit — came very quickly.'

'You didn't get the number plate?' Sam asked.

'No, but there should be enough CCTV to get it.' Jamal shook his head. 'That's the way it works on the TV, anyway.'

'There's no CCTV in this street,' Sam said.

'No, but whichever way you go there will be some on one road or another, I'd have thought.'

'And you've heard nothing since?' Letty asked.

'Not from the police, and the woman

hasn't been to her office since. I'm waiting to see if she turns up tomorrow and everything's all right.'

'Let's hope,' Letty said doubtfully.

'Except,' Jamal said, 'it's not all right for your friend, I assume.'

'We haven't heard from him,' Letty said.

'He was mixed up in something,' Jamal said, looking from one to the other of them.

Letty nodded. She liked Jamal but there was no way she'd be able to explain exactly what they were mixed up in.

'Shall we exchange numbers and let one another know if we find anything out?'

As they did so, Jamal lowered his foot to the floor to walk to the door with them.

'I expect a visit to update me if you're only across the road,' he said, looking at Sam. 'I'm going to have this on for another few weeks, and you make a decent cup of coffee.'

Sam nodded. Despite the shock, Letty didn't fail to notice that Jamal stood at the door to watch them go — and that Sam glanced back at him with a half-smile as she and Letty made their way down.

13

Letty and Sam were silent as they crossed back over the road and didn't speak until they were back in Sam's office, which felt even messier after the bright, airy space they'd been in.

'Well,' Sam said. 'That was like being in the theatre. It's entertaining — fun, even — and then you come out and realise Adam has been punched and forced into a van.'

'Two days ago. He could be anywhere by now.'

Neither of them said it. *He could be dead*. Letty couldn't trust herself to say any more, she was struggling not to cry and her hands were shaking.

She took some long breaths.

'Should we go to the police? They already know what happened because Jamal's told them but at least we can put a name to the man who's caught up in it. And explain the background.'

'I wonder how interested they'll be at this stage. They'll be more concerned about the child and I don't think anything we've got will help trace them, will it?'

Letty shook her head. 'Probably not.' She couldn't even really point any fingers as to suspects. She didn't think it was Nate Wickham himself who had done all that — and if the police spoke to him about it, he could be spooked and flee sooner rather than later and then they'd miss out on getting him for his past crimes.

'Perhaps I'll tell the private detective,' she said. 'He's been working on the old case that Adam's aunt was involved in and we met him the other day. If he could give the police everything he knows it would put the kidnapping in perspective.'

Sam's phone sounded to tell her there was a text for her. She picked the phone up.

'Jamal,' she said. 'He says *Look at local news*.' She went quickly over to her computer. She moved the screen so that Letty could see it as well as she found the website.

'Police are asking for information about a missing four-year-old thought to have been abducted near the town centre,' said a voice-over as an image of a small boy was shown, and another of the street where he was last seen. Their street.

Then there was a video that was difficult to see clearly as it was dusk. A van answering the description of the one that had been present where the boy was last seen had been spotted some distance away. On the CCTV footage, when it drew up, the back opened with a jerk and a figure appeared.

'That's Adam,' Sam gasped.

Letty watched as Adam sat down at the back of the van, legs dangling, and lowered himself down to the road. The little boy was clasped in his arms and clinging to Adam. It made it difficult to run, but run Adam did. Towards the camera and past it. As he passed the camera, a vehicle overtook him and began to nose in front of him.

The voice-over said that police were particularly interested in tracing the driver of this vehicle. 'The driver might have realised the child was being abducted and tried to stop the perpetrator.'

'What?' Letty and Sam both said, aghast at this interpretation.

'Is it possible to go back, see all that again?' Letty asked.

Sam made some movements with the mouse and they were back at the image of the child.

'Can you pause that?' Letty asked as the video began. 'That could be almost anywhere and we don't know what time it was, but it's possible it's the street where Adam's aunt lives. There's the residential block on one side and they're doing some building opposite, behind a fence.'

'They said it was less than an hour later,' Sam said. 'How far away is that place?'

'Oh, ten or fifteen minutes' drive from here, I suppose. No more.'

'What was happening for the rest of the time?' Sam looked worried. 'Though, I suppose, well, Adam doesn't look as though — you know . . .'

Letty knew what she meant. As though he'd been beaten again. 'No. You can't see his face properly but he gets down OK and he can run.'

They were silent for a moment.

'Can we try to see what colour that car is? Do you think it's really trying to stop him?'

It was impossible to say with any certainty what colour it was or what the driver's intention was. It was a dark colour, anyway.

'What's he got in his hand?' Letty asked as they watched again.

Sam froze the screen and juggled with the zoom. It wasn't clear. Letty didn't want to say what she thought it was.

'It looks like a hammer,' Letty said eventually, her voice shaking.

'So it does.' Sam grabbed the mouse again. 'Look, the back door looks quite dented as it opens there. He's bashed his way out with a hammer.' She looked at Letty. 'Go Adam,' she said admiringly.

'But if he's escaped, where is he now? And the little boy?'

Letty's phone sounded and she wondered if someone she knew had seen this report, but it was an ultra-short text from Fede.

She stood up. 'Adam's aunt is back at her flat. I need to speak to her.'

Sam stood up as well.

'I wonder if that's where he'd make for if he saw that's where he'd landed up.'

'No, he thinks she's in London. Anyway, he'd think it would be a dangerous place to be. I don't know why Rowena's gone back.' She picked up her bag. 'Thank you so much for all this, Sam. It's still horrible but we're clearer than we were. I have to call a taxi and get round to talk to Rowena.'

Sam was switching the computer off and collecting her own things.

'I've got my brother's car this weekend. I'll drive you there. Don't worry, I'll wait outside.'

* * *

There was a car parked opposite Miss Kemp's block of flats.

'Do you mind not parking too close to that car, Sam? A navy blue car keeps cropping up when bad things happen.'

'Do you think that might be it?' Sam manoeuvred her brother's car into a space on the other side of the road some distance away where they could see both the blue car and the entrance to the flats. 'Actually, do you think it's the one from the film?'

'It could be, couldn't it? Or it's just somebody's who lives here.'

'Want me to come in with you?'

Letty did. Her insides felt hollow and her legs wobbly.

It was a Sunday, she reminded herself. People would be at home cooking, eating their lunch, reading the newspapers or watching a film. Someone would come out if she shouted.

Sam opened the glove compartment and closed it again. Letty felt for the door handle. Even if Sam found a hammer for her, she wasn't sure she'd be able to use it against anyone.

'No — better not complicate it. Rowena might not speak freely if there's someone she doesn't know there.'

'Sure. I'll keep watch.'

'I'll put my phone on silent. Let me know if anything happens or — or if you have to go.'

'I'm not going anywhere.'

Letty smiled a shaky smile and headed for the front door.

The lift was at the second floor and going up, according to the lights on the ground floor. Letty took the stairs. If someone was in the lift, they'd only see her if the doors opened at the floor they got out of. She could hang back until it was safely past and continue going up.

If they were walking down, she'd meet them without warning. At best, if she heard someone she could hover at the entrance to the flat situated diagonally opposite to where you got out of the lift and might go unnoticed.

She just had to hope for the best.

The lift stopped at the fourth floor. Someone got in and went down.

When she got to the fifth floor, there were voices from the floor above and Letty almost lost her nerve.

She could run back down. She didn't want to put Rowena in danger, after all.

It was only one voice — a woman. She was pressing the button repeatedly to call the lift while talking on the phone.

'I can't get in. They've changed the bloody lock.' It sounded as though she was trying to lower her voice but not having much success. She sounded angry. 'I know you told me to leave it but I don't like untidy ends and you wouldn't either if it came back to haunt us. It's always me who has to do the clearing up. Who are you talking about? What do you mean, the boy?'

Letty sensed that the lift wasn't coming back up and hoped the woman wouldn't stop trying to call it and start walking. She was desperate to see if she had a blonde wig on, but couldn't be sure that woman wouldn't know who she was.

She twisted her hair round in some semblance of a pony tail and tucked it into her clothes. If the woman did know her, at least the blonde hair flowing down her back wouldn't be such a giveaway.

'Taking the boy as well was a mistake, I admit, but it wasn't his fault. Your son does everything you tell him to, which is quite a lot. What do you mean, it's me who asks it? Are you going to put all this on me? Come on, Ethan, it'll only be another week and we'll be out of it, starting again.'

Ethan! So it could be Maria up there. The voice sounded different.

Letty got ready to sprint to the far flat and turn her face to the door.

'What are you saying?' It was as if the woman upstairs was standing still, shocked at what was being said on the other end of her phone.

'It's next week we're leaving. Stop joking, Ethan. You're not on your way now. You can't be! That's not what we planned. Anyway, I've got the papers from the office you asked me to go and get — you said you can't go without them.' Maria, if it was her, was not being cautious at all and her voice rose. 'So why did you send me to pick them up?' There was a short silence. 'All right — I can join you tomorrow . . .' The calm was short-lived. 'What? What?' she squeaked.

Letty so wished she could hear the other side of the conversation.

The lift clunked its way up and drew to a stop on the sixth floor.

Letty thought the woman — Maria? — was crying, or trying not to cry. This was not how Maria would act, but if she was on the phone to Ethan she would still be a person of interest to the police.

She had to do something. She couldn't get past and into Rowena's flat without this woman seeing — and within a minute she would be down on the ground floor and gone.

Letty remembered that moment when she was left on the central reservation in London because she hadn't moved quickly enough. That didn't matter in the end — indeed, it meant Fede could approach her unseen and in terms of where she was going it cost her and Adam a minute, no more. But this wasn't the moment for hesitation. The stakes were much higher.

Letty breathed deeply, and moved. She flew down to the first floor and waited till she could hear the lift coming down.

It was a long shot. They'd have got it fixed after Adam reported it that time. It had probably been a fluke fault that day. This might not have been how it happened.

She tugged at the gate on the first floor and it opened a fraction.

The lift clanked to a halt. It was just above her head and she could hear a wail.

'Now I'm stuck in the bloody lift. Don't go without me! No, I only got them to board that part of the house up. No point in attracting attention. This is how I solve problems for you. All of it, Ethan? What do you mean, the whole house is boarded up? Why would you do that? Where are we going to bloody live for the next week?'

Maria never swore. That's why she hadn't thought it was Maria's voice.

'Don't bloody go to Heathrow without me.'

Maybe Pamela Marr swore. It could have been Pamela Marr in there. Maybe the reason Maria didn't chat much was because she was changing her voice as well as her appearance.

That would be exhausting. No wonder the strain was showing.

Letty raced up again and tapped at Miss Kemp's door. 'Rowena, it's Letty,' she called softly and the door opened as if Rowena had been standing just inside it. She had the pistol in her hand and Letty tried not to react.

'Pamela Marr is stuck in the lift. I opened one of the gates a fraction and it stopped between floors. Could you call the police? And can I take some of your paper to put *Out of Order* signs up? I don't want anyone to free her unknowingly.'

It all came out in a rush.

‘Oh, well done.’ Rowena got paper and marker pens out. ‘The police are on their way — they’ve been waiting round the corner.’

Letty picked up a pen. ‘Why have you got a gun in your hand?’

‘It’s not a real one.’ Rowena laughed. ‘What have you done to your hair?’ She looked remarkably relaxed.

Letty stared at her former teacher, hardly able to believe her eyes. Three and a half weeks ago they’d sat and talked about shorthand outlines and Sherlock Holmes. So much had happened since then.

‘All they have to do is close the gate on the first floor and the lift should start up again.’ She picked up her notices and ran again.

When Letty got to the bottom, having stuck up all the *Out of Order* signs and a *Danger — do not touch* one on the first floor, she ran out to Sam’s brother’s car. Sam wound the window down.

‘I haven’t spoken to her yet,’ Letty said breathlessly, ‘but I think someone who came to finish her off is stuck in the lift. She's on her way down anyway and Rowena is safe. I hope the police are coming.'

'Will she know where Adam is, this woman in the lift?'

Letty had been so wrapped up in the urgency of the events that had unrolled she had forgotten Adam for a moment and now the fear came flooding back.

'I'm just going to have a quick talk to his aunt. She may know something, and if not, there's one other place to look. Do you want to go? I promise I'll let you know what's happening.'

'No fear.' Sam laughed. 'I'll wait and watch here and then drive you to your next place.'

'OK — or if you like, you can come into the building and lurk at the bottom to see if Pamela gets out of the lift.'

Sam was out of the car in a flash.

'And if she does?'

'You say 'Good afternoon' and watch which way she goes. But hopefully what you'll see is the police rushing in and then leading her out in handcuffs.'

'What does she look like?'

'Middle-aged, middle height and she may or may not have a blonde wig on.'

'I'll recognise her, then.'

The gun was nowhere to be seen when Letty got back to the sixth floor, out of breath. There was a smell of coffee and toast and Letty's stomach rumbled. Rowena, in the kitchen, gestured to mugs and plates.

'Jon Walters thought Ethan Marwick was coming to finish me off. I came back here to make it easier for him. Well, as we saw, it wasn't him, but I didn't feel like breakfast until they'd gone. Will you join me?'

'Yes, please. Isn't Fede here?'

'No. He wanted to be but in the end we thought that if someone did get in, they'd be less likely to be encouraged to talk if they thought someone else was here.'

'Did she try to get in? Weren't you taking a risk?'

'She's a clever woman in many devious

ways but she didn't realise I'd change the locks after someone got in with the keys. We had an interesting conversation through the door, though.' She signalled to Letty to sit down and start eating and went across to a small device. 'Jon gave me this. I wonder if it came out all right.'

There was a bit of static and then it started, one side somewhat muffled but audible.

— *Rowena, let me in. We need to talk.*

— *Who is this?*

— *Pamela Marr.*

— *Who?*

— *Ethan Marwick's wife.*

— *What do we need to talk about?*

— *Your nephew. We've got him.*

Rowena didn't reply — whether to force Pamela to say more or because she was shocked wasn't clear. Then she spoke, clear and unwavering.

— *Let him go. He's nothing to do with any of this.*

— *Any of what?*

— *Ethan killing Derek Rawlings.*

— *I just want to make sure the past is*

past. You need to let Ethan alone now.

—Why do you think I have any influence over what happens now?

— It was all your idea, prosecuting Ethan. You kept the papers. You know your nephew has lost them? Probably lost more than that as well.

There was a pause and in the recording Letty could hear Rowena breathing, as though she was struggling to keep calm.

— The papers aren't important, Pamela. Ethan can keep all the money he tricked people out of. It was killing Derek I can't forgive him for.

— He didn't even do that.

Pamela's voice was getting shrill, the tone Letty had detected outside.

— So long as he ordered it and paid for it, he's guilty.

—You don't know anything.

— Tell me, then.

— Let me in. We can't talk properly like this.

— It was you, wasn't it?

Letty's eyes opened wide, breakfast

forgotten. It had been Maria behind it all the time?

Rowena switched the recording off. 'Get on with your toast, dear.' She stood up. 'I should have offered you peanut butter or something.' She fetched a jar and a clean knife. Letty dug in.

'I think she's lost control,' she remarked. 'I know this woman as Maria Palmer and she's very calm and controlling.'

'Yes, Jon mentioned that you worked with her.'

'Did she say where Adam was?' Letty asked.

'No. When I told her if Ethan had done nothing wrong I'd make sure the case didn't go ahead, she denied ever having him. It was just a trick to make me hand over whatever I had.'

'She was on the phone to Ethan outside and it sounds as though they were planning to leave the country anyway.' Letty wiped crumbs from her lips and hands. 'I have to go.'

'Why did you come, Letty? Fede said

you wanted to talk about something.'

Rowena's phone rang. She listened for a moment and agreed to something.

'The police are on their way up now,' she said. 'They've arrested Pamela. Is there some information you want to give them?'

'There's something else I have to do first,' Letty said, hurrying to the door. There was no point in telling Rowena that Adam was missing after all. She'd look in one last place and then hand it all over to the professionals. 'Thank you very much for the coffee and toast. Let's speak soon.'

Rowena stood at the door looking calm but a little confused as Letty, hearing the lift about to arrive, hurtled towards the staircase.

14

'What did you say the street was called?' Sam slowed down to try to get a glimpse of a plaque with a street name.

'Tanninghall Close.' Letty peered at the map on her phone. 'It's saying it's this one.'

'They're nice houses.' Sam sounded admiring. 'I've never been here before.'

'Nor me.' Letty laughed. 'I've never known anyone this well off. Oh, look, it might be this one. Yes, turn left.'

There was no other traffic. Sam stopped, backed up, signalled left and turned into a wide street of elegant detached houses.

'We don't want to stop right outside, do we?' she said, slowing down. 'Let's try to see what the numbers are.'

'I might have to walk up one of the paths. The doors are too far away to see.'

Sam continued peering out of the window.

'No, look, there's a number on a gate there — twenty-two, is it? And the one next door has put the bins out and it says it on them — twenty. What number do we want?'

'Fourteen. Stop here.' Letty felt overwhelmed by the grandeur of the street. She knew Nate Wickham was doing well, but these houses had to be worth two million or more. 'I'm so glad you're with me, Sam. If I'd come by taxi I'd be feeling very vulnerable out here on my own.'

Sam smiled. 'If I wasn't here, I'd only be filing.'

Letty pointed. 'We might be OK to get closer. If I'm counting right, number fourteen is the one that's boarded up. Now I come to think of it, Maria might have said something about the house being closed, or part of it anyway.'

Sam started the engine and drove slowly to the house in question. Boards covered every window and the front door.

'And they were going to leave the

country,' Letty added.

'That's not what you'd do, though, is it?' Sam mused, gazing at it.

'No.' But Ethan and Pamela didn't do things the normal way. 'I might just have a walk round to look at the back.'

'Suppose there's someone guarding it at the back?' Sam said.

Letty got her phone out to make sure it was still on silent in case she were to come across someone as she looked around the edge of the house. There was a message from Terry.

Good news. Midnight back! Turned up today tired and hungry but fine. So happy.

That was good news. If Nate was leaving the country today, he could release anyone he'd been holding. He'd got what he needed from Terry, an assurance Terry wouldn't shop him, and could now let the hostage go. He'd be somewhere else, someone else, tomorrow. Letty was so happy for Midnight and for Terry's family.

And that meant Adam would be let go, didn't it? It had to. This was all going to be a wild goose chase.

'Want me to turn round and get ready to leave quickly if there's anyone else there?' Sam asked.

Letty gave a strained smile. 'You're taking to the role of getaway driver very well.' She was pleased with the escape plan if one were needed, and happy to have Sam's support.

She walked through the gate and across the front lawn. There was a wall on either side. To one side of the house there was a garage and to the other, an alleyway with a wooden door to get through to the back garden. She scrambled on to one of the bins, up onto the wall and hooked first one leg and then the other over the door. The wall continued on the other side and it wasn't that far to jump down.

Odd they hadn't boarded this side gate up. There was a bolt top and bottom, and she pulled them across quietly so she could run through quickly if there was any danger in the back garden.

The windows at the back, however,

were boarded up as well. There wasn't a security guard anywhere to be seen, but Letty still couldn't breathe properly.

At the end of the garden was a summerhouse and she walked gingerly across to look in. She didn't dare look up at the houses on either side. These properties had a reasonable amount of space around them but if anyone was watching, they'd see her.

The summerhouse didn't smell well used. There was just some garden furniture, a big toolbox on a wheeled trolley and a few new-looking suitcases. That would be the last thing she did — look inside the cases. Her imagination was running riot and she wished she could get the image out of her mind of what could be in there.

Would you leave a body, or body parts, in the house where you'd be the first suspect once it was found? People like Nate and Maria would do anything, she supposed. If they were going to change their identity again and start in another country, they might think they could get away with anything.

They had done before.

There was an extension built on the side of the house behind the garage and if anything, the plywood covering these windows was thicker. There were waste pipes as well, as if this was another kitchen and bathroom. A utility room and downstairs cloakroom, perhaps? Or a granny annexe. It certainly hadn't been for Dawn Marr, and it was odd to think of the slick businessman Nate Wickham having a parent he cared about enough to bring them to live with him. Stranger things happened, she supposed, but, if she'd ever lived there, Granny wasn't there now.

Letty jumped as Sam appeared by her side.

'Nothing?' Sam asked and when Letty shook her head she went on, 'I've just been talking to the neighbour. Nathan left this morning, the neighbour said. Nathan told him he was flying off tonight, didn't say where to. It sounds like the neighbour complained to him about having the house boarded up like this, said it lets the street down, and Nathan promised to get someone on to selling it as soon as he could.'

'Interesting. Did he say when the wife left? I'm not sure what name she'd be calling herself.'

'Before Nathan, he said. She organised the carpenters to board up the annexe this morning, apparently, but he didn't talk to her — finds her a bit difficult, he said. Then she went off somewhere in her car and Nathan spoke to the carpenters. They went away and came back with more wood and boarded up the whole house. That was when the neighbour stepped in to complain.'

'He was keeping a close eye on things,' Letty commented. 'Your chatty informant.'

'He and his wife couldn't believe what was going on. Never seen the like, by the sounds of it.' Sam laughed. 'He should have lived where we did, growing up. Half the houses were boarded up at one time or another. Oh, and he said Nathan left his wife's stuff in suitcases in the summerhouse.'

'What, the neighbour was supposed to tell her when she got back?'

'It did rather sound like that.' Sam pointed to the wall where Letty was standing. 'Do you suppose that's the annexe?'

'I was thinking that's what it is. And it does look more . . .' *Fortified*, she wanted to say, but that wasn't the right word.

'It's certainly well boarded up.' Sam looked it over as if hoping for a way in. 'Another funny thing the neighbour said was, the banging had gone on for so long, his wife could still hear it — even once they'd all gone.'

Letty looked around the garden. Most of the containers were too heavy to lift but she hoisted a smaller one, thick and solid-looking, and knocked it against the board on what would be the kitchen window of the annexe. She had to turn it in her hands several times to get a good enough grip to be able to really make a noise with it and used all her strength.

On the fifth knock the pot broke into three in her hands.

She shoved the plant and broken pieces on the nearest flower bed. As she straightened up she yelled, 'ADAM!' at the top of her voice.

Sam jumped with surprise. Letty knew she was giving the neighbour something else to complain about but she wasn't ready to give up yet.

There was a yard broom propped against a trellis and Sam grabbed it and rammed the end of it against the wood as if it was a battering ram. Letty wasn't sure whether the purpose was to make a hole and get in, or make anyone inside hear. Or just desperation to do something. Letty could sympathise with that feeling.

'ADAM!' she called again.

After a moment she put a hand on Sam's arm to stop her furious banging and they heard a tapping inside. It sounded like tapping. That, and what could have been someone clashing pots and pans together. Or it could have been the neighbour making Sunday lunch . . .

She was prepared to risk looking foolish if that was the explanation. The easiest thing, she thought, would be to hope Rowena was still with the police — explaining all this to someone who didn't have the background would be difficult.

She didn't know whether Rowena even knew her nephew was missing yet. If Letty didn't tell them, the police wouldn't know. Hopefully it was going to be good news before the afternoon was over — but this wasn't the way to tell her. She got her phone out.

'Have you got a police officer with you?' she said. 'I'm at Ethan Marwick's house and he's locked someone in the granny annexe. Could they come?'

She gave the address, then ended the call and ran to the summerhouse and grabbed the toolbox to see whether there was anything that would help them.

She felt like trying to hammer her way through, but levering the nails off might be a better idea. They weren't weathered in yet.

She started at the bottom, prising nails off one by one. It was hard work but mercifully they popped out. After a while, Sam took over.

'It's taking for ever,' Letty complained.

Sam puffed and carried on levering the boards away.

Trying to stem her panic, Letty walked around to look at the front of the house and saw blue lights flashing and a group in blue uniforms trying to break the front door down.

Maybe that was a better idea.

Sam, sweating now, passed her the screwdriver and she saw glass where the boards had been prised off. The window was cracked but it was clearly Adam inside the room, looking shocked.

She could have cried with relief.

'Hang on, Adam!' she called.

The child in his arms was clinging on tight, as he had in the video, but now his little face was pressed tight against Adam's shoulder.

By the time the whole window was

uncovered, two policemen had found their way round to the back garden. Adam was leaning across the kitchen sink trying to open the casement window. It was difficult because it needed two hands, but he got there.

'Pass the child out,' one of the police called.

Adam spoke softly to the boy, who shook his head and held tighter. Still murmuring as if to reassure him, Adam tried to stretch up to hand him through the window but the child wailed and wriggled, still not showing his face.

Adam shook his head. 'He's a bit upset. Could you stand back for a minute?'

The two men quietened. Maybe they were family men. Or maybe they'd had to deal with situations like this before.

Letty kicked the toolbox over to the window and stood on it.

'Might he come to me?' she said softly. She was shaking.

'Letty, love, what on earth are you doing here?'

'Getting you out.' She felt like

laughing, but felt so sorry for the child and all he'd been through. And anxious about what Adam might have been through. 'What's his name?'

'Petey.'

'Hello, Petey,' she said gently. 'I'm Letty. Do you want me to help you out into the garden? Then we can get you home.'

At least he looked up.

'Is my mummy there?'

'No, but there are some nice policemen and women who can take you to her.'

'Not the bad man and the shouty woman?'

'They're not here, Petey. You're safe now. Can you crawl towards me and get through the window?'

Adam put Petey down on the draining board and steadied him.

Petey turned his head back to the room as he crawled out. 'Are you coming, too?'

'I'll be right behind you.'

Letty reached out for the child. He

was surprisingly solid and heavy in her arms but he let one of the men take him from her, and this man put him gently down in front of Sam.

'Will you get Adam out now?' he asked Letty anxiously.

Letty caught Adam's eye and grinned. 'You bet. That's why I came.'

But in the end Adam didn't need to crawl out of the window into her arms — not that it would have been like that because she would almost certainly have dropped him, she reflected. The police came through the internal door.

All around her she could hear discussion of how long the air would have lasted as she ran round to the front door and through the house to Adam.

She leaned against the kitchen table, shock setting in. She thought if she didn't sit down she would fall down, but Adam took hold of her until she stopped trembling.

'It's OK, Letty,' he murmured against her hair. 'Everything's all right now.'

He held her until someone separated

them. He didn't have any words. She couldn't articulate her own relief and gratitude either — but she had a sense this wasn't finished.

She held on to Adam's hand until the last possible minute. Then someone led her back through the darkened house and out of the battered front door and took her to one side in the front garden. A woman police officer started to ask about her role in what had happened that day. She watched as a uniformed officer spoke to Adam, snapped a pair of handcuffs on him and led him away.

She interrupted the question the policewoman was framing. 'No, you can't take that man,' she protested. 'He was abducted himself. It wasn't his fault the child had got into the van.' She let out a sob. 'He's the real victim. He looked after the child.'

'It will all be clarified at the station, I expect. Now, you were first on the scene here today. Who does this house belong to?'

'Someone I work for at Nate Wickham

Accountancy Services,' she said reluctantly. It probably wasn't sensible to try to trade her information for Adam's freedom. No one would believe for very long that Adam had taken Petey, surely. 'He used to goby the name Ethan Marwick but now he's Nate Wickham. And I think his wife lives or lived here too. She's either Maria Palmer or Pamela Marr.'

'Right — Pamela Marr. She's in custody now.'

'I believe the husband is on his way to Heathrow now, ready to fly out and change his identity again.'

The policewoman called to her superior and Letty overheard the decision that they should head for the airport.

'Do we have a photograph of this man?' the superior officer asked. 'How do we know who we're looking for?'

'I know what he looks like,' Letty said. 'I'll go with you.'

15

Letty sought out Sam, still in the back garden. 'I've said I'll go with them to the airport to identify the guy who lives here. Will you be all right?'

'Sure. Go. I'll find Adam in a minute and see if I can give him a lift home.'

'I think they've taken him to the police station.'

'Of course, that makes sense. I have to go and give a statement later, so I'll catch up with him there.'

You never knew whether new people you met gave and accepted hugs but Letty opened her arms to Sam anyway.

'You've been amazing,' she said gratefully.

Sam hugged her too. 'We've done all right.'

'We have.' Adam's arrest would be sorted out by the time Sam got to the station, surely. It wasn't another lie not to mention it to her now.

'Good luck at the airport.'

Letty nodded and went back to the front of the house.

'Which terminal are we headed for?' the driver asked once they were on the M25, she and three plain-clothed officers with another car behind them.

'Do we even know where he's on his way to?' another of them asked.

'I can only think possibly Malta,' Letty said. Of course, she hadn't considered the size of the airport.

The man beside her, who reminded her of Terry and who could probably mingle unnoticed in a busy terminal, made some phone calls and reported back there were no flights to Malta that afternoon.

Letty didn't know if she imagined it or if the driver took his foot off the pedal slightly. It was true, there would be no point hurrying if they were going to have to comb all the terminals.

'They could see if they could get it out of the woman they have in custody,' Letty suggested. She hadn't watched all those cop shows for nothing.

The detective, who announced himself as Gary on the phone, made another call, but without urgency.

Letty closed her eyes. She felt empty and her rushing thoughts stilled for the first time in days. All this, to be foiled at the last minute because she hadn't got all the information. Even if Pamela knew where he was headed, and would tell the police, Nate Wickham could be someone else by tomorrow.

And into the quiet, a memory emerged. She opened her eyes and sat up straight.

'Unless there's a flight to Bermuda. He mentioned Bermuda.'

There was a buzz of calls and tapping of phones then, 'Bingo. Bermuda, twenty-oh-five from terminal three.' She felt her body sucked backwards as they sped up again.

* * *

They were met by a number of uniformed police, who stayed at the entrance. Only the plainclothes officers went into the terminal with Letty. It felt as though it would be like looking for the proverbial needle in a haystack as they entered the terminal. Letty's brain switched off again. She followed the three of them towards the queue for the Bermuda flight and they stood looking at her.

She tried to concentrate. Would he look different on a Sunday, when he was escaping one life for another? Had he already organised his disguise? She forced herself to examine all the passengers, from the front to the back of the line. She shook her head slightly but new travellers were joining the end all the time. It was difficult to focus. There wasn't enough air, and there was too much hubbub.

'I'll get us entry to Departures,' one of the detectives said. 'In case we've missed him.' He stepped aside and got his phone out.

Letty was worried about losing sight of her three companions and glanced behind her to make sure she'd still be able to alert them quickly if she spotted him, although the expectation of spotting him was fading. There were too many people.

Then, there — just behind her as she turned — was not Nate, but someone else she recognised.

'Claire?'

'Letty.' Claire looked confused. 'What are you doing here?' She'd gone very pale. 'Don't tell me he's taking you instead.' She glanced over Letty's head and Letty thought there was recognition in her eyes. She turned around and there was Nate, just a few metres from them.

Gary was beside her immediately, watching and listening. Letty lifted her chin slightly in the direction of where Nate stood, still looking around, oblivious to what was going on. 'Tall slim guy,' she said softly. 'Dark grey jumper, short hair.'

'I see him.' Gary signalled to the other two.

They must have some sort of unspoken code, Letty reflected, because they closed in on their prey like an experienced pair of predators.

'And the woman?' Gary asked.

Letty nodded. 'She's nothing to do with any of it but it looks like she was going with him.'

Claire was moving away but appeared stunned and allowed herself to be arrested as well. That explained Nate's odd comment yesterday. *You won't want to upset Maria next week*.

Letty felt strangely empty. She should be feeling elated. Adam was safe — and Rowena too, if Ethan Marwick was in custody.

She felt sad for Claire, but Claire knew what she was doing. She must have understood the deal when she packed her bags and made her way here. She must have been planning this since the day she told Letty she wouldn't want not to have her nieces in her life. She evidently decided that whatever Nate could give her was more important.

Terry had been right. Claire was much further in than Letty could ever have imagined.

It wasn't over, though — because if it was Nate's son who had hit Miss Kemp and abducted Adam, he would still have to be found. She wondered if Adam would be able to describe him. If he was really only about twenty, he may not have a criminal record. He would be able to disappear.

From the corner of her eye she saw a young man in a leather jacket watching what was going on. A large backpack sat at his feet and one hand rested on it, as though he was on his way to the queue and had put it down for a rest. Or as though he was looking for someone. His phone was in his other hand. She didn't know whether she was inventing a resemblance to Nate . . .

'What?' Gary was quick to understand. He must be a great detective, and someone good to have around in a fast-moving situation. Or maybe she was too transparent — he could almost read her thoughts.

'See the guy in the leather jacket

watching Ethan being taken away? I think he might be the son.'

The boy seemed to come to a decision. He hoisted his backpack and started to make his way through the crowd. He was easy to follow as the bag was so big — and there was so much going on, he wouldn't have noticed as Gary made a phone call.

The boy hesitated once outside the building and two uniformed police officers came up either side of him and started talking to him. Just questions, by the looks of it, but he wouldn't have been able to make a run for it.

Letty and Gary stood watching, and a police car made its way to the taxi rank. Rucksack and young man were put inside.

'Suppose he was just a random backpacker who realised he'd come to the wrong terminal and is going to miss his flight?' Letty asked.

Gary burst out laughing. 'I don't think they would have taken him if that was remotely likely.' He put a hand gently in the small of Letty's back. 'Let's you and I find ourselves a bad cup of coffee and gather our thoughts,' he said. 'We've missed the last car out for a while anyway.'

Letty didn't think to check her phone until they were approaching home. The faithful Sam had updated her:

Having pizza with Adam, Rowena, a tango teacher whose name I can't remember and Petey's aunts and uncles. Everyone very pleased with you. Adam identified his captor as soon as he saw him and Petey picked him out from photos so all looking good.

A second one that was sent an hour later read:

Adam exhausted so we won't wait for you. Seeing Petey's mum in her office tomorrow at 11 — if you are not at work, join us?

* * *

Letty was early the next morning — she couldn't wait to see Adam. They'd both been too exhausted for explanations the night before, but each messaged to say they were OK. Now she had that slightly anxious feeling again. Adam had been through such a lot. There was no way he wouldn't be affected.

Nor her, to be honest. Things weren't just going to go back to normal straight away. There would be the court case. There was always the risk justice wouldn't be done, but she thought the case must be strong now.

Fortunately Adam was early too and was on his own in the office, which was still chaotic, with the new cabinets still to be filled.

He let her in and closed the door behind her, then opened his arms wide. It sounded like a cliché to say she fell into his arms but that was what it felt like. Rushing into his arms and being held up.

'I am so happy to see you,' she mumbled against his shoulder.

He looked better than he had the day before.

'I'm so happy to see you,' he said. He held her for a moment longer then loosened his hold so they could talk better.

‘Letty, I have to go across to speak to Petey and his family in a minute but we’ll have time to talk, won’t we? A bit later?’

‘All the time we need.’

He hugged her tight again. ‘You saved us both,’ he said, his voice husky. ‘You saved our lives.’

Letty blurted out what she’d been worrying about all night.

‘It wouldn’t have happened if I hadn’t insisted on digging and digging. Rowena was right for the wrong reasons. You should have kept away from me.’

‘No, no, no.’ He shook his head. ‘Letty, darling, no. Then it would never be over.’

Darling. He called her darling. He wasn’t sorry she’d meddled in his family’s affairs.

‘The police would have got you out anyway.’

‘No, I’m not having that.’ Adam laughed. ‘I had pizza with everyone last night when the police had finished with us all, and while you were making sure everyone got arrested. Aunt Rowena and Fede are very clear that it was you who made sure all this ended as happily as it has.'

'Do they think the police will be able to make a good enough case against them?'

'Aunt Rowena does. She's seeing Jon Walters today and thinks we may need to talk to him as well.'

'That's OK.'

Adam approached the door and put a hand on the handle. 'Are you OK to go across now?'

'Yes. Or do you want me to wait for you here?'

'Not at all. Petey's mum wants to meet you.'

Letty's phone began to ring.

'Take that,' Adam said. 'We said eleven and it's not that yet.'

'It's Terry,' she said. 'From Nate's office. He's probably wondering where we all are.'

'Letty, love.' Terry sounded strangely cheerful. 'We've got the police here and I'm wondering if you're coming in. Nate and Maria have gone, just like I thought they might, but now the police have turned up and they're here searching everything.'

'I wasn't going to, Terry, but I could — later. I'm in the middle of something now but we probably need to talk.'

'We do, but there's no hurry. I just wanted to let you know there's a certain amount of excitement in the air here because some of the consultants want to carry on with the company. Along different lines, of course, but I wanted you to know in case you're out job hunting.'

'I'm not. And that's interesting.'

'Everyone's shocked, of course, but mourning the loss of Nate and Maria lasted about five seconds. We'd need some legal advice, but I must say I'm excited myself.'

'Me too now, Terry. I may know a legal adviser.' Letty looked at Adam and he raised his eyebrows.

'Great stuff. Claire's not here and I can't get in touch, so I'm wondering if she knew what was going to go down and is lying low. She may be interested in this too.' When Letty didn't answer

Terry went on, 'Anyway, no hurry, love. Come and see me either in the office or at home.'

'Will do, Terry. Thanks for letting me know.'

She crossed the road with Adam.

'The workers want to take over Nate's company,' she said. 'That was the deputy. He was surprisingly keen.'

Adam looked at her with a smile. 'You sounded surprisingly keen yourself.'

Letty chuckled. 'I surprisingly am. It's very early days and may turn out to be a bad idea but I don't remember when I was last so excited about a job.'

It felt as though she would be helping to start something from scratch and she felt sure Terry would want her to have a say in shaping it.

Petey, his parents and older brother were just arriving as Adam and Letty reached the entrance to the block over the road. Petey broke away from his family and threw himself at Adam.

'How's my little buddy?' Adam bent down to hug him.

'All right, thank you. I missed the end of the pizza.'

'You were asleep, weren't you? Was it nice to get into your own bed?'

The little boy hesitated.

'I slept with Mummy and Daddy,' he said.

'Good idea,' Adam said. 'I bet they liked that.'

Petey smiled and glanced up at Letty.

'You got me out of the window.'

She crouched down too.

'You were brave, stepping through.'

'Then the lady with the jibjab gave me some water. She's coming today, too.'

Adam stood up, laughing.

'One of my many failures over the weekend was not being able to get him to say hijab.'

Letty smiled and straightened up too. 'I bet Sam loves 'jibjab'.'

'Thank you both for looking out for my son.' Petey's mother stood in front of them with one hand on Petey's head. She was near to tears as she turned to Letty. 'You're the one who found them, aren't you?'

'I made a lucky guess.'

The woman hugged her.

'May your whole life be lucky.'

'Is Petey OK?' Adam asked as the little boy ran off to play with his brother, under the watchful eye of their father. 'Did the police mention getting him someone to talk to?'

'They did. But it would have been so much worse if you hadn't been there, Adam. I can't believe they'd accuse you of taking him, after all you went through as well.'

'Well, the handcuffs didn't stay on for long!' Adam reached out for Letty's hand but still addressed Petey's mother. 'Did you know we were drugged for a while?'

'Yes, so the police doctor said, but it was through his system by then.' The woman wiped away another tear. 'He said when he woke up you were in a dark flat together and that you got him to bang pots and pans together.'

'I had no idea where we were. We could have been in the middle of nowhere, or somewhere someone would hear it. It kept him occupied, if nothing else.' Adam smiled. 'I just hope he doesn't think it's all right to do that in your kitchen now.'

'I get that the 'bad man' is the one Petey saw hit you and bundle you into the van,' Petey's mother said. 'But where did the 'shouty woman' come from?'

'She was in the blue car that stopped us when we managed to get out of the van.' He lowered his voice. 'She was actually more frightening than the thug with the fists because she seemed out of control.'

'She's the one who drugged you both?'

'I guess so. She nearly ran us down in her car — the car actually knocked into me and I was carrying Petey, so I rolled over to keep him from going on the ground. Then she got out, shouting and waving something around and I couldn't get us both up quickly enough to run for it. The next thing I knew, we were in the house and I don't really know how much time had passed.' He turned to Letty. 'The police worked out that the original plan might have been to get me into my aunt's flat and make her agree to drop the case.'

'She wouldn't be able to do that, though. I heard her tell Pamela Marr it was out of her hands.' Letty thought for a moment. 'I wonder if she'd stopped thinking clearly by then.'

'I think you're right there.' Adam looked at Petey's mum. 'I could give you my phone number in case things come up you need to ask. It's all credit to your family that Petey is so resilient but . . .'

'Yes, thank you. Shall we go into my unit to talk?' Petey's mum suggested hesitantly. 'There are a few people there working but . . .'

Letty could see why Adam wasn't offering to have everyone in his. That wouldn't be comfortable either.

After a moment Letty realised that little Petey was staring at a man coming out of the main door of his mum's office building. Of course the child would be fascinated by the orthopaedic boot.

It was right he was here. Jamal had

enabled them to set all this in train. He should be updated.

Introductions were made. 'We should go into the office, Adam, however much of a mess it is,' Letty said quietly. 'Jamal can't stand in the street for long.'

'You could come up to mine,' Jamal said.

'There are a lot of us,' Letty said.

Jamal grinned. 'You've been there,' he said. 'I've got a lot of space.'

They all went inside, slowly to accommodate Jamal's pace.

'Is Sam coming?' he asked.

'She's on her way,' Adam said.

Jamal looked pleased. 'Only so she can make coffee for us, you understand.'

Letty caught his eye. 'Of course,' she said.

They would make a stunning couple.

She reached for Adam's hand. That was even more news he needed to catch up with. Although when Sam herself arrived, carrying pastries and doughnuts, and Adam saw them together in Jamal's kitchen, she thought he may be able to work that part out for himself.

It turned into quite a party, and Letty began to feel warm and contented inside. She knew she and Adam would do a lot of talking. Miss Kemp had some explaining to do as well — not least how to do names in shorthand.

Letty glanced across at Adam, laughing now with Petey's father.

Letty had been looking forward to life settling down, but she realised that wasn't going to happen. She might help Terry start a new company — that would be fun and both of them would have ideas on how to keep it a healthy workplace. But more importantly, she and Adam had been through a lot together and she wanted to get to know him properly.

A new life with Adam Taylor. Now that was a risk she was fully prepared to take.